THE PANTY THIEF

ANNETTE MORI

ALSO BY ANNETTE MORI

Pleasure Workers
A Window to Love
The Book Witch
The Book Addict
The Dream Catcher
Free to Love with Ali Spooner
Unconventional Lovers
The Organization with Erin O'Reilly
Captivated
The Termination
The Review
The Ultimate Betrayal
Locked Inside
Out of This World
Asset Management
The Incredibly True Adventure of Two Elves in Love
(Affinity 2014 Christmas Collection)
Love Forever, Live Forever
The True Story of Valentine's Day
Vampire Pussy..Cat
Nicky's Christmas Miracle X3
(*It's in Her Kiss*, Affinity's Charity Anthology)
Who is Nicolas Claus
(Christmas Medley 2017)

THE PANTY THIEF

ANNETTE MORI

Affinity
Rainbow Publications

2019

The Panty Thief
© 2020 by Annette Mori

Affinity E-Book Press NZ LTD
Canterbury, New Zealand

1st Edition

ISBN: 978-1-98-858845-2

All rights reserved.

No part of this book may be reproduced in any form without the express permission of the author and publisher. Please note that piracy of copyrighted materials violate the author's rights and is Illegal.

This is a work of fiction. Names, character, places, and incidents are the product of the author's imagination or are used fictitiously and any resemblance to actual persons living or dead, businesses, companies, events, or locales is entirely coincidental

Editor: Angela Koenig
Proof Editor: Alexis Smith
Cover Design: Irish Dragon Design
Production Design: Affinity Publication Services

ACKNOWLEDGMENTS

A huge thank you to all of my beta readers: Gail Dodge, Carrie Camp, Ameliah Faith, Dana Holmes, Elle Hyden, Danna Micoletti and Maria Siopsis who made great suggestions to improve the initial draft. As always, I have to acknowledge Erin O'Reilly who is a constant support and encouragement to me. I am honored to call her a friend and have her support me in my journey.

I would also like to express my gratitude to Affinity Rainbow Publications and the wonderful trio (JM Dragon, Erin O'Reilly and Nancy Kaufman) who continue to provide feedback to tighten up manuscripts that need assistance and publish my unconventional work. I am eternally grateful for the opportunities they give me to let my stories see the light of day.

My other family members who are also very supportive include my nephew, Aaron, and his wife, Chelsea, my older sister Val, and my father who struggles to read my books with one eye.

I always enjoy working with the beta editor Nancy Kaufman who helped tighten my story. Thanks to Angela Koenig for her magic as the final editor to tighten the story even further. She is a delight to work with. Inevitably, there are those pesky final errors that slip through and I am thankful that the final proof editor, Alexis Smith, caught those before the book went to print. Thanks to Nancy Kaufman for the final cover. Nancy is also a promoter extraordinaire. Huge thanks to all the other readers and fellow writers who have sent personal e-mails, written reviews, and posted nice things on Facebook (you know who you are). The Affinity authors are an especially supportive group and often share posts or send words of encouragement. Finally, my wife, Jody, continues her support even when it interferes with our time.

DEDICATION

To Sophie Lennox who was the inspiration to this story and the spark for "Panties Week." And, as always, to my beautiful wife whom I love with all my heart.

TABLE OF CONTENTS

PROLOGUE

The sinewy naked body slipped from under the covers in catlike grace as the owner was careful not to disturb her sleeping companion. She'd waited until she heard the tiny snores, which were a telltale sign she could make her move.

Knowing the exact spot where her prize had landed, she hurried to the place beside the bed where the lacy red thong lay innocently on the floor. She snatched the underwear in one hand and grabbed her jeans, also on the floor, in the other. After stuffing the panties in the pocket of her jeans, she pulled them over her tight body. She didn't bother to don her own underwear. There wasn't much time before she risked the woman waking and catching her. Too much was at stake if the beautiful woman awoke to find her not only stealing away in the darkness, but literally stealing her expensive lingerie. She didn't know the exact cost, but this pair was not her normal run of the mill stolen pair.

Already making her move she gathered her T-shirt, socks, and underwear and finished dressing. She shoved her own panties in her other jeans pocket after pulling out her cash and tossing a twenty on the dresser. Pausing before muttering a hushed "shit," she added another twenty to the lonely bill. She hoped that would be enough. Pushing the rest of the bills back into her pocket, she was ready to make a quick getaway. The bulging pockets might stand out, but she wouldn't worry about that. People minded their own business in the city.

The thief knew she'd never see the woman again. In a city as large as Seattle, the chances were unlikely. Even if she ran into any of the women by chance, they never suspected she was the one who had stolen their panties. Who would sleep with someone and nick their underwear? That would be a fetish to record in the *Journal of Modern Psychology*. She chuckled to herself. Her one-night stands would never assume that had happened. She'd always played it safe, but the thief wondered when her luck or the one-night stands would run out.

Careful to open the high-rise apartment door soundlessly, she breathed a sigh of relief when she was on her way. Pulling her smartphone from the back pocket of her jeans, she used the Uber app to call for a ride and make her way home.

As the thief waited for her ride, she vowed that this would be the last time she would do this. She tried to convince herself the theft was more a tradition and not an obsession or addiction. She could stop anytime she wanted. In fact, she could forego another one-night stand too. Stress sometimes increased her activity. Soon her stress would subside and she'd be able to laugh about the indiscretions of her youth.

Grinning to herself, she thought of her apartment and her dresser where all the other prizes lay stacked inside. She had a special place in her drawer for her treasure after she washed them. Her fetish did not extend to keeping someone's unwashed panties in a trophy drawer. That was gross.

CHAPTER ONE

Sabrina thought about the day she'd met Joey Hartford. She should have known Joey was trouble and would lead her right into a life of crime. Okay, maybe what she'd done didn't constitute a life of crime—hyperbole on her part. And yet, technically, it was a crime. Joey was stealthy; Sabrina had to give her that. Perhaps she'd paid a little too much attention to that slyness, and that had allowed her to act with abnormal confidence. The thrill was dangerous. Addictive. She wouldn't continue on this path. Especially not now that things had changed between them.

The basement of the apartment complex had been more than a little stuffy, but at least the pleasant aroma of dryer sheets and detergent filled the air. The older buildings in

Seattle had that musty smell with a hint of unhealthy mold in places the naked eye couldn't see. That resulted from living in a city that rained most of the time. Glancing around the room she noted the off-white walls with multiple black scuff marks.

The building was old and in need of a few repairs. Repainting the walls would be a start if they had any hope of brightening up the place. The complex was all she could afford until she finished school. A barely discernible hum of the dryers lulled her to sleep. The only thing keeping her awake amid the soft whine of the machines was the uncomfortable hardness on her behind and against her back from the industrial plastic chair. Maybe she would bring a reclining lawn chair next time. The loud ding on the dryer would be her alarm.

Bent over the washing machine in the old apartment building, Sabrina was pulling out her wet clothes. She stuffed them into the gigantic dryer designed to hold two loads. When she turned around, there Joey was.

Joey had carelessly slung a duffel bag over her shoulder. The corner of her mouth lifted, ever so slightly. It wasn't just her lopsided smile that reminded Sabrina of a cross between a leer and a smirk. Would someone call it a *smeer* or a *lirk*? Sabrina was always making up new words. She liked mashing things together. The clincher was Joey's penetrating eye contact and the languorous movement as they took in every inch of Sabrina's body. Sabrina couldn't control the delicious shiver up and down her spine. Joey's smoky gray eyes made Sabrina want to push her up against the dryer she was leaning against. She was a sucker for bedroom eyes. Forget the come-fuck-me pumps, she preferred women with come-fuck-me eyes.

"You're new," Joey had stated.

Sabrina could barely respond with her one-word question. "What?"

"I know every fine ass in this building. I would have recognized yours."

"Huh?" Sabrina was more than a little shocked. She had on her workout sweats. They weren't at all flattering. Her unruly hair kept falling in her face as she blew hard at the strands. Frustrated, she absently grabbed a fist-full of hair and pulled the fly aways back into confinement. Wrapping the hair tie three times to keep her hair controlled, she blinked.

Joey shrugged. "You have a nice ass. I got a good view while you were bent over."

"That is about the rudest, most misogynist thing I believe I've ever heard. I didn't think women could be misogynist pigs, but you've blown that theory out of the water."

"Well, I subscribe to the *honesty is the best policy* philosophy on life. Women should be more honest. It was a compliment. When you hit fifty and we're planning to go out for the evening, I'll be honest if you ask me whether your ass looks big in a nice tight skirt."

Sabrina crossed her arms over her chest and glared. "I don't wear tight skirts. In fact, Ms. Misorude, I don't wear skirts at all."

"Misorude?" Joey had looked perplexed, her face pinched in confusion.

"Yeah, a cross between a misogynist pig and rude person."

"Hmm, beautiful and clever. Okay, forget the tight dress then. I'll be honest about your ass in a snug pair of jeans. Better?" Joey dumped her duffel on the ground and pulled her dirty clothes out. Sauntering to an empty washing machine, she tossed the clothes inside. She hadn't bothered to separate the colors. "I'm Joey," she called over her shoulder as she glanced at Sabrina.

"Sabrina." *Why am I giving this rude woman my name? Because she's hot. Now who's the misogynist pig?*

Startled from her thoughts, Sabrina watched Joey strip, removing her jeans, T-shirt, and socks, flinging them unceremoniously into the large, white, industrial machine with scratch marks on top. Sabrina approved of the eco-friendly detergent she retrieved from her bag.

Wide-eyed, Sabrina blinked, but continued to stare. Joey had a sports bra and the sexiest pair of boi shorts on that Sabrina had ever seen. Airbrushed models didn't rock the look as much as Joey. Her height came from her legs, but she was also long-waisted which meant there was a great deal of toned flesh beneath her bra and above the top of her underwear. Sabrina's mouth went dry.

Joey did that *smeer* thing again and then raised an eyebrow. "Like what you see, Sexy Sabrina? You know that messy hair thing is absolutely working for you. Kinda reminds me of what a person looks like after mind-blowing sex."

"You can't just strip in the community laundry room. What if somebody else comes down here?"

"So? Geez, you'd think I was naked." Joey filled the coin slots and turned the dial to start the machine. "What I'm wearing covers more than some of those bimbos show on a beach with their butt floss thongs masquerading as bathing suits. I like to make the most of my load of laundry and my precious time. I can think of a dozen things I'd rather be doing than laundry. But, it's a necessary evil if I don't want to offend someone with my rank smelling clothes." Joey slammed the lid and hopped on top of the machine, swinging her legs.

The heat rose to Sabrina's face as she asked the next question. "Um, are those—" she pointed at Joey's boi shorts "—comfortable?"

Joey blessed Sabrina with a wide smile, not her lopsided grin that Sabrina thought was a bit arrogant looking. "They sure are. I don't like when bikini briefs ride up my ass. Although, I have to admit that nothing beats commando. I save that for the weekend. Sometimes. It depends on what I have going. My dates like seeing me in my boi shorts." She waggled her eyebrows.

"You're really going to sit here in your underwear and wait for your clothes to wash and dry?"

"Uh huh. Unless you're offering to babysit them for me. I have a helluva study session to return to but I needed a break. Laundry seemed like a good choice. Sex would have been better, but I'm fresh out of new coeds to exploit." She continued to sit on top of the machine with her hands on either side bracing her while she leaned forward.

The swoosh and thump of the washer seemed muted with Joey's tall body muffling the sound. Sabrina noted how Joey's torso did not change as she leaned forward. It was just as flat as when she had stood earlier like a Greek goddess.

She shook those thoughts from her head as Joey's words registered in her brain. Then she pursed her lips and mumbled, "Pig."

Joey held up her hands with her palms facing outward. "Kidding. Well...about the coeds, not about how beneficial sex can be in reducing stress."

"You say every little thing that pops into your head, don't you?"

"Refreshing, isn't it?"

"Not the word I would have chosen. What are you studying?"

"Medicine. Final year of med school and it's a real bitch. It's never too early to prepare for the boards, but my real focus right now is the Step Two Medical Licensing Exam. Soon enough things will get better for me when I start my clinical rotations."

"I hope you aren't training to be a cancer doc. I don't think they will appreciate your brutal honesty."

"Au contraire. When you're dying, you want the straight up truth, not a bunch of medical mumbo jumbo. At least that's what my mom wanted in her final months. She didn't get it from anyone but me. Thank fucking God she did, too. I helped her cross off every item on her bucket list. I was the one to introduce her to one of my friends so she could have the real deal on a lesbian experience. Mom was hot, and it thrilled my friend to hook up with her. My father, bless his heart, accepted her need to do everything she hadn't experienced before, even that. Just between you and me, I think he thought it was hot, though they both refused to have him watch."

Sabrina wrinkled her nose. "Ew. I can't imagine my mother having sex, much less sex with one of my friends."

Joey shrugged. "You get over a lot of the 'ew' in life when faced with the reality of losing a parent at an early age. Petty everyday life shit doesn't matter anymore." Joey hopped off the machine and turned away.

Sabrina thought she saw a small crack in the abrasive veneer. "I'm sorry about your mom."

"Circle of life." Joey turned back to face Sabrina and the left-over unshed tears were visible. "New topic. Do you work or go to school?"

"Both, I guess. I'm finishing my doctorate while working at an outpatient mental health facility." Sabrina continued to stand as she answered Joey. She wasn't sure whether to return to her hard-plastic chair or continue the unusual conversation with both of them standing in the middle of the room.

"Interesting." Joey relaxed against the large washer and scrutinized Sabrina.

"It is. I could lecture you on how our whole system of healthcare is failing because of the insufficient resources for mental health, but I'll spare you." Sabrina tucked back a strand of hair that had escaped her hair tie once again. "Listen, I could watch your laundry for you. Give me your phone number and I'll text you when they're done. I can toss them in the dryer for you."

Joey chuckled. "Smooth. Is that your tactic for obtaining phone numbers? You know, you didn't have to think up any pretense, I would have gladly given you my number."

"Um, I wasn't...really that was not my, uh..."

"Relax, Sabrina. I was teasing. Although, I would like to take you up on your offer. There are not enough hours in the day to accomplish everything. If I devote the next couple of hours to studying that will allow me the free time to take you out to dinner tonight."

Sabrina blinked twice and stared at the woman clad only in her underwear. She wasn't sure if she'd heard correctly. Was this hot woman asking her out?

"You can say no, if that's why you haven't answered yet." Joey frowned. It was the second time Sabrina had glimpsed something other than the confident, aloof woman.

Sabrina rushed to answer, not liking what she thought was disappointment plastered on Joey's chiseled features. "No, no, that's not it. I was trying to work out in my head whether the dinner invitation was a date."

Joey's face transformed and the tiny lopsided grin appeared. "Perfect. Text me later, Sexy Sabrina, and we can finalize the details." She held out her hand and wiggled her fingers at Sabrina.

"What?" Sabrina scrunched her face in confusion.

"Gimme your phone and I'll program in my number."

"Oh, okay." Sabrina pulled her phone from her pocket and handed it to Joey.

Joey started typing and chuckled to herself as if she'd made an especially funny joke. She handed the phone back to Sabrina after she'd finished and then dug into her duffel to pull out a fist full of coins. She stepped closer and placed them into Sabrina's palm, and then lightly stroked her wrist while looking into Sabrina's eyes. "You are far too beautiful for my self-preservation. If I travel to the other side unscathed, it will be a miracle."

Sabrina watched her walk away and had an irrational desire to remove the boi shorts clinging to her shapely rear end. She wanted to try them on. To see for herself if they were as comfortable as Joey claimed. The bonus would be Joey without a stitch of clothing on. She'd have to remove the sports bra. She was never any good at that. The bane of any lesbian's existence was a tight sports bra. That normally killed the mood when you were trying to impress your partner. Details. Tiny details for her full-blown fantasy.

†

Joey hadn't expected to find anyone in the community laundry room so early on a Saturday morning. Few people were early risers in the building that housed students and a few young professionals.

She didn't know every person in the building, but she knew most of them. Her neighbor across the hall and an occasional friend with benefits, Maribel, had mentioned there was a new woman on their floor, but Joey hadn't paid a lot of attention to the idle gossip. Maribel had remarked on how attractive this new person was and had pinged her gaydar. Although, she wasn't sure why because the newbie didn't scream lesbian. Maybe it was the eye contact. A look that lasted a fraction too long. If that perusal was followed by an obvious, or in Sabrina's case not so obvious, cruise of her body, that clinched the assessment.

Sabrina was a lesbian, especially with her comment about trying to figure out if dinner tonight was a date. A very attractive lesbian. Tiny ringlets of auburn curls kept escaping from her messy ponytail and framed a heart-shaped face. Long lashes outlined Sabrina's large, intelligent, hazel eyes, something Joey had focused on when Sabrina had let them roam over her body. Had she cruised Maribel too? Joey didn't like that Maribel and Sabrina might have eyed one another.

Joey's thoughts returned to her future. Her final year of med school was challenging at best. A tit buster at worst. Sleep and free time were almost nonexistent. She counted on the generosity of Maribel to help her relieve the occasional stress she felt. She was one of the lucky ones who didn't have to worry about school loans. A job was waiting for her after she finished school. Sure, the job was in a rural area that provided care to an underserved population, but that was a small sacrifice in exchange for a debt-free life after medical school.

Joey sighed and returned to her studies. She couldn't afford to squander her time daydreaming about Sabrina, when later tonight she'd drink in every last drop as Sabrina joined her, in the flesh, for dinner. A knock on her door interrupted her foray into internal medicine. Joey groaned in frustration. She did not need this disruption.

Maribel stood in her doorway, grinning. Maribel was stunning with her long blonde hair, blemish free complexion, and pouty, naturally red lips. Add to that her curvy body with large, perky breasts and she was every person's wet dream—man or woman. She had a kind of raw sensuality that sucked a person in. Long curvy lashes accentuated her light brown eyes. An unusual combination that added to her appeal.

"Hey, gorgeous." She held up a white bag. "I brought treats. I thought you might need brain food and some exercise to start your day out right. It's never good to harbor all that stress when studying. Too many days have gone by. Let me be your release valve. I love when you study in your undies. It must be laundry day. Aren't you afraid someone will steal your unmentionables?"

"Not today, I don't have time."

Maribel brushed the tips of her fingers over Joey's chest and pouted. "Aw come on. The day is still young. You have plenty of time to return to your boring studies."

Joey caught a whiff of the sweet-smelling items in Maribel's bag. She had to admit that freshly baked goods were always tempting when the aroma penetrated one's senses.

"They aren't boring to me. I don't have time for this, Maribel. Seriously. And pastries are not brain food. How many times do I have to tell you that?"

"Someone's grumpy today. Fine, maybe I'll introduce myself to the new girl. She's hot."

"Don't do that. Keep your fangs away from her."

"Why? Are you jealous or something? Don't worry, Joey, you'll always be my number one fuckbuddy."

Joey rolled her eyes. "Suit yourself. Feel free to knock on her door at"—Joey turned her wrist to look at the time— "eight-thirty. You know most of the people in this building don't emerge on a Saturday until well past ten. Why are you up? I thought vampires slept during the day."

"Funny. I know you're an early riser and I was horny this morning, after waking from a wet dream where you were the star. It was worth a shot. Fine, I'll just head back to bed now and finger fuck myself. Call me later if you want to have a little fun. I'm taking my pastries with me. Toodles." Maribel turned and walked away after giving Joey a small wave.

Joey breathed in relief. She'd narrowly averted disaster. She wanted to keep Maribel away from Sabrina. There was something innocent about Sabrina and the last thing she needed was corruption from Maribel. Joey had barely resisted the offer of drugs that would allow Joey more hours in the day. Maribel had assured her the stuff was guaranteed to keep her awake. She'd insisted it was a myth that humans needed greater than four hours of sleep each night. Joey was functioning with five to six hours, but the constant lack of sleep was taking its toll on her after four years. She was glad she'd never surrendered to temptation. At least, not that temptation. She was only human. Other temptations were far too difficult to avoid. Joey was convinced that Sabrina was at the top of that list. If only she'd turned around the minute she'd spied that fine ass and run for the hills.

She sat back at her desk, flipping through her textbook as she sipped on her coffee. She made a deal with herself. If she buckled down without another intrusion for the next couple of hours, she would allow herself more interaction with Sabrina when the text came to retrieve her clothes. Dinner tonight would not be enough time, and a few more minutes wouldn't make much of a difference in the grand scheme of things. Quality study breaks were important. She'd heard a lecture once on stress and time management. The lecturer insisted that after a certain point, the law of diminishing returns played a significant role in the effectiveness of study time. Study breaks and brain food allowed for more efficient use of those precious twenty-four hours allotted to a person each day. All-nighters were not the way to go.

†

The loud buzzer from the dryer startled Sabrina from her daydreaming. She hated to admit that she'd been thinking of Joey standing there in her tight boi shorts that clung to her ass like a second skin. She had imagined Joey stalking her and taking charge as Joey pushed her down on the bed and kissed her. The kiss wouldn't start tentatively. No, it would be rough and full of passion. Joey wouldn't bother with buttons. She'd rip off Sabrina's clothes to touch her bare skin.

Sabrina shook her head. She could not, no she would not let herself go there again. It was always the attractive ones that triggered her obsessions. When she'd moved to Seattle it was supposed to be a new start for her. But what was the harm in a little fantasy?

As she removed the warm clothes, the lavender scent from the dryer sheets wafted in the air, adding to the already faint smell of the room. She would toss in a few of the sweet-smelling sheets when she transferred Joey's clothes to the dryer. She hoped Joey would appreciate the clean scent as much as Sabrina did. Her hands smoothed over the final T-shirt she'd folded. The laundry basket was now brimming with clean clothes.

The extra-capacity washing machine dinged and Sabrina walked over to remove Joey's clothes and begin the final process. The number of boi shorts in the load of laundry was astounding. "Twenty-two, twenty-three, twenty-four, twenty-five, twenty-six," she counted out loud. *Who has twenty-six pairs of underwear compared to four T-shirts?* This didn't make a lick of sense to her since Joey had admitted that she didn't don underwear every day of the week. Sabrina maybe had ten pairs, and she never went commando. She wondered if Joey would miss a small item of clothing. She had a naughty thought as she pondered stealing just one pair. Surely Joey wouldn't notice one missing pair of boi shorts.

Sabrina held up the teal pair in her hands and noticed a picture of a woman peeking through what looked like a torn piece of paper. The ironed-on picture appeared on the ass. Scrawled at the top was the word "Captivated." Wait a minute. This was the cover of a book she'd read a few years ago. Sabrina wondered why Joey would have a pair of underwear with the cover of a book on the butt. She'd have to ask her about it at dinner. Strange. Sabrina reached into the dryer and pulled out a few of the other pairs that had a splash of color on either the front or back side. She wasn't sure why she hadn't noticed them before while counting. Six of the pairs had various covers from the same author. Was the author her girlfriend? Wife? She would most assuredly ask about it now. Sabrina was not a home wrecker.

She tossed the pair into the machine, added two dryer sheets, and closed the door. It was ridiculous to consider taking a pair, especially one with a logo or cover art. Sabrina had to admit that thinking about being some kind of panty thief was exciting. She'd always been a good girl and stealing underwear was naughty in so many delicious ways. She grinned and settled onto the plastic chair with her tablet thinking about her almost wave of crime. The book she was reading was okay, but it helped pass the time. Reading was better than fantasizing about a woman she could never have. She wondered what she was doing having dinner with Joey tonight. Sabrina didn't do one-night stands, or two, or three. Not anymore. Her perspective had changed from the early days when she'd first discovered she was a lesbian. She vowed not to fall back into that pattern. And she wasn't interested in being the other woman. Sex was a vague remnant of the past.

It had been a long year since her breakup with Carolyn and she couldn't believe the wound still felt a little raw. Charming Carolyn. She could wiggle her way into anyone's heart in a matter of minutes. That was the problem. She'd infiltrated more than one person. Man. Woman. It didn't matter to her. Carolyn was bi-sexual or gender fluid and that hadn't made a difference to anyone. What mattered was her need for newness. Sabrina ceased being new after their first year. By their fourth year, she was barely her roommate. Her roommate who paid the bills. Discretion wasn't a strong suit for Carolyn. Sure, they were both young when they met, but sometimes people settled down with their high school or college sweethearts.

Sabrina clung to the intermittent rewards that Carolyn flung in her direction. A romantic gesture here. A night of hot, wild sex there. Those tiny morsels kept her alive until she brought her indiscretions into their bed. Enough was enough. Sabrina could not get past the sight of Carolyn's head between one of their closest friend's legs. The loud moaning was the final straw. The sight and sound of that evening haunted her still.

Carolyn had insisted it was nothing. Just sex. Couldn't Sabrina understand that love and sex were two different things? She'd cried and said she loved Sabrina. Insisted she would get help and change. Sabrina took her last ounce of self-respect and moved across country to start anew. She understood more about addictions and illnesses now. Several years of an immersion into her studies solved that problem. Her compassion allowed her to forgive Carolyn, but not forget.

Shaking her head, Sabrina returned to her book. She sensed another person's presence before hearing the clip clop of shoes on the hard, black-and-white checkered flooring. The scuff marks were starkly vivid on the white squares. An attractive woman was staring at her.

"Hey. I saw you the other day. You're the newbie in 5H." She glanced at Sabrina's full basket, nodded, and then grinned. "Looks like you're done. How come you're still hanging out in this stuffy room?"

"Um… I offered to finish—"

"Joey. You met Joey. I knew it. She sweet-talked you into doing her laundry. Didn't she?"

"Uh...no. I offered. It was my idea." Sabrina sat up straighter in her chair.

"Sure it was. Want some advice?" the woman asked.

"Not really." Sabrina felt her irritation rise. This stranger would not tell her anything she didn't already guess was the brutal truth. Getting involved with someone like Joey was a terrible idea.

"Suit yourself, but Joey, well, she's an emotional vampire. She'll suck the emotions right out of you and leave a vacant husk behind. You'll be no good for anyone else after she's done with you."

"I'm doing her laundry, not fucking her." The biting edge to Sabrina's voice and use of profanity surprised her. She wasn't sure why she felt the need to explain herself. "Who are you anyway? A jilted lover?"

"Nope, not jilted. I'm Joey's occasional stress reliever. Maribel in 5B. I live across from Joey and down the hall from you. You know, you're exactly Joey's type. Bet she already asked you to dinner." Maribel lifted herself onto the machine across from Sabrina and crossed her legs as she settled in.

Sabrina wondered about the wisdom of moving into this new building. Capitol Hill in Seattle was a nice place to live. She enjoyed seeing so many other lesbians, but the drama she could do without. Not to mention how old and run down this building was. She didn't consider the building as on the par with the projects from back home, but it wasn't modern and shiny either.

"Look," Sabrina began. She would use her calm voice, the one that worked with clients who unraveled. "If you and Joey have something going, I'm not interested in getting into

19

the middle of any dyke drama. That is the last thing I need or want."

Maribel cocked her head. "What are you? Some shrink or something? You have a shrink voice."

Sabrina sighed. "Sorry. Occupational hazard. No, not a shrink yet, but I slip into the role more often than I should. How about we start again without the contentiousness that a mutual acquaintance seems to have caused? I don't know Joey or you, but I'd prefer to be friends versus enemies. I've read about neighbors who are enemies and I don't want any part of that." Sabrina stood and stuck out her hand. "Sabrina. Truce?"

Maribel chuckled and clasped Sabrina's hand in both of hers. She stroked the inside. "Another friend with benefits. Why not? You're kinda cute with that messy ponytail and tiny dimples. Yeah, and I bet you clean up real nice."

Sabrina shook her head. "Sorry, I don't do the friends with benefits thing. Not judging at all. It's just not my thing."

"Ah. You're one of those. That's cool. Mashing sex with love works for some people."

"I sure hope so. I'm still looking for that other person it works for." Sabrina laughed.

Maribel smiled. "Broken heart, huh? I get it. If I had a heart to break, I suppose I might feel differently. You're okay, I guess. For now," Maribel added.

It almost felt like an afterthought, but Sabrina caught the undertone.

"Give Joey my love. See ya around, dimples." Maribel pivoted and strolled from the room without looking back.

Sabrina shook her head and sat back in the chair, pondering the new challenges on the horizon for her. Maribel gave her the creeps. Something was off about her. Sabrina couldn't quite put her finger on it. Maybe it was the smile that didn't quite reach her eyes. Or perhaps the sharp edge on her words. A little too crisp. This was a woman used to getting what she wanted, and when she didn't, her mood spun on a dime. No matter how hot Joey was, Sabrina would clarify that getting in the middle of whatever was between her and Maribel was out of the question.

CHAPTER TWO

Joey's leg was bouncing up and down. Her restlessness was getting to her after checking her watch every five minutes. She'd expected a text message from Sabrina by now. And yet, nothing. Pushing herself up from the chair, she decided she wasn't getting much done wondering about Sabrina. Before she made it to the door, she heard a quick knock. Grinning, she yanked on the door, expecting to see Sabrina, but instead came face to face with Maribel. Her face lost the joy it held as her smile vanished.

"What do you want now? I told you I'm busy." Joey adopted a tone of boredom. Never anger, because that might set Maribel off and she wasn't in the mood for drama.

"Met your girlfriend. She's cute in that wholesome, vanilla sex sort of way. I bet she won't even muff dive on anyone. A pillow princess for sure."

"You went to the laundry room." Joey was cautious. Maribel was unpredictable. She could either suggest a three-way or fall into a rage she would swear wasn't jealousy. It hadn't been much of a problem for Joey because she didn't have a lot of time for a social life. The occasional fuck with Maribel met her needs for the time being.

"You're predictable, Joey. Saturday is laundry day. I figured you met Sabrina this morning and conned her into doing your laundry. Did you ask her out?"

Maribel tried to sound casual, but Joey could hear the carefully engineered tone in her voice.

She took a chance with her response, hoping Maribel wasn't sitting on a powder keg this morning. "None of your business."

"That's a yes. I don't think she's into threesomes, but if you asked, she might agree." Maribel leaned against the doorframe and adopted her sexy pose. This normally encouraged an invitation from Joey, but not today. Something was distracting Joey.

"I'm not into threesomes, Maribel. You know that. Threesomes are your thing, not mine."

"Pity. I'm sure we both could show her a thing or two. Go ahead, have your little stroll over to the fluffy white clouds and when you're ready to return to the dark side, come see me. I'll be waiting." Maribel pushed off the door frame and walked away. The slight sway to her hips was tempting, but not tempting enough for Joey to become embroiled in her sex games today.

Joey decided it was time to see how her laundry was doing and if Sabrina had escaped her interaction with Maribel unscathed. She felt oddly protective.

†

Peeking around the open door, Joey made sure that Maribel had returned to her apartment before sneaking back to the elevator that would take her to the laundry room. She stabbed the button marked B with a little too much gusto. The elevator groaned and creaked like an old woman. Joey wondered if one of these days, the elevator would stop working—much like people did when they got too old and their organs gave out. Her anxiety was manifesting itself in her index finger. She curled and uncurled her hand, attempting to shake off her feelings of impending disaster. When the elevator dinged, she hurried to the laundry room and caught Sabrina pulling one of her boi shorts from the dryer and scrutinizing the pattern on the front.

"Like what you see?" Joey interrupted Sabrina before she was sure the sexy woman was about to bring the underwear to her nose for a sniff. Kinky. Maribel was so off the mark. Although, Joey thought, people with a panty fetish usually sniffed underwear before they made it through the wash.

Sabrina bobbled the boi shorts in her hands and they fell to the floor. She jumped. "Shit, you scared me. Why do you have twenty-six pairs of briefs? That seems like overkill. And why are there book covers ironed onto the front or back?"

Joey laughed. "An author friend of mine thought it would be funny to slap, 'Free to Love,' 'Captivated' and 'Dream Catcher' on the ass or"—Joey pointed to her crotch—"vay-jay-jay. I agreed and asked her to print me some. Besides, I now have more than enough underwear to last several months without doing laundry. I'll admit to wearing my T-shirts, shorts, and jeans more than one day, but I draw the line at undies. And I suppose I've collected a few others over the years after...oh never mind. Hey, you don't have to fold my clothes."

"Oh, I'm almost done. Folding laundry is therapeutic for me, so I didn't mind finishing this for you. Um...about dinner..." She leaned over and picked up the boi shorts she'd dropped on the floor.

"No, no, no, no. You can't cancel on me. I know you met Maribel, but we're not together. I swear. We're friends with occasional benefits."

"It's none of my business but I don't think Maribel can decide on whether she doesn't like you at all or likes you too much. I believe it is the latter and I'm not interested in drama, particularly dyke drama. I'm also not interested in friendship with benefits or a one-night stand. I know that works for some people and it's cool. Non-committal sex is not something I'm into," Sabrina's words rushed out without an intake of breath.

"You eat, don't you?"

"Yeah."

"Dinner is about food. I wasn't offering sex. Food and conversation that's all. I swear. I gotta eat and take periodic breaks and you gotta eat. Oh, and for the record I don't have phobias around commitment."

Sabrina raised her eyebrow. "Really? Me thinks the fair maiden doth protest too much."

"Right now, I only have time to commit to one thing, medical school. And trust me, I am very committed to her.

She's a nasty jealous bitch when I don't pay her enough attention and the consequences aren't pretty. Don't presume to know anything about me from a short ten-minute discussion over panties."

"Still, in my line of work, I can recognize those skating on the edge. Maribel seems obsessed and you, unfortunately, are the object of her fixation at the moment. Big yellow caution lights are flashing all around her. If I agree to dinner, we'll have to reframe the evening. Not a date. Okay?"

Joey held her hands in the air in a placating gesture. "Deal. Dinner. No date. Two people sharing a meal in the most unromantic place we can find. Burger Hut work for you?"

Sabrina continued to fondle the underwear she still had in her hands. "No fast food, please. Somewhere with quality food. Maybe off the beaten track. A hole-in-the-wall that everyone underestimates at first glance."

Joey thought Sabrina intended the comment and glance as a double meaning. An apology perhaps for misjudging Joey and underestimating her.

"Speaking of obsessions, you seem focused on my underwear. Do you want a pair? I have plenty to spare. I wouldn't want you to turn into some depraved panty thief."

Sabrina blushed. "No thanks. I think I can afford to buy some of my own."

"But they won't have one of these pretty pictures on the ass." Joey held up a peach pair of boi shorts with an abstract painting of a woman and *The Dream Catcher* in bold print.

"True. Tempting, but no. I wouldn't want to owe you something. And I'll be paying for my dinner tonight."

Joey scooped the folded and unfolded clothes into her duffel. "I'll come by your apartment at six. Will that work?"

"Sure." Sabrina picked up her basket, and they both walked side by side to the elevator.

Joey pushed the button while Sabrina carried her full basket in front of her. They parted ways when the elevator doors opened. Joey risked one last glance at Sabrina's backside and mumbled, "Yep, very fine ass," right before she caught Sabrina turning her head and looking down the narrow hallway at Joey.

†

After returning to her apartment, Sabrina had scanned her phone to find the new contact, Delicious Boi Shorts. She'd laughed and changed the name to Joey. She would have to get Joey's last name to complete the contact. Only Joey would be brazen enough to type that in. Joey was a cocky little shit, but there was something about her that intrigued Sabrina.

The almost tentative knocking on her door surprised Sabrina. But what threw her for a loop was Joey standing in the doorway tugging on her fitted button-down shirt. She wore black pants that clung to her body in a way that showed off her assets without looking cheap or overly sexualized. *She's nervous.* The observation made Joey endearing. No doubt Joey was intelligent, sexy, and charming. Her raw vulnerability that occasionally appeared made her irresistible to Sabrina. She could relate to the forgotten people who needed someone to care about them. And she clamored to develop a closeness with those most vulnerable. Wasn't everyone vulnerable in some small way, no matter who they were or how well their life was unfolding before them?

For all Joey's protests that this wasn't a date, but two people sharing dinner and conversation, her selection on attire for the evening suggested otherwise. This time, the shoe was on the other foot and Sabrina blurted out the first thing that came to mind, "Don't get me wrong. You look scrumptious, but that"—she pointed at Joey—"is not what I would call casual attire for a non-date dinner."

The lopsided grin appeared on Joey's face. "Boundaries, rules, and anything else that screws with the small amount of fun I allow myself are far too tempting to demolish. We won't do anything you don't want us to do tonight. I promise."

Sabrina shook her head and grabbed Joey's arm slipping hers inside. "Come on, take me to this great place before I change my mind. It's a good thing I'm starving."

"Maybe I should renegotiate the terms of our agreement while your brain lacks the sustenance required to make good decisions. What's the harm in calling this a date? It'll make a fine story for our grandchildren."

"Nope, I will not be your tawdry mistress. Medical school is a formidable opponent. I'll bide my time and see how things work out between you two. Hopefully, you'll part on amicable terms when your relationship comes to its inevitable conclusion. I'm a trained therapist, you know, and I can tell when relationships are doomed."

"I always remain friends with my exes. It's the lesbian way."

†

Sabrina looked around the small cafe featuring wood fire pizzas. The place was trendy, but casual. Joey led Sabrina to the farthest booth from the front door and motioned for her to sit. The almost black, solid wood booths showed wear and tear, with a fair number of dents and scratches. Classic red brick surrounded the place and kept the interior darkened, but cozy. The bricks were old and almost crumbling in some places. Behind the bar was the only light-colored item in the joint—a half wall with the same dark mahogany wood sitting on top.

What stood out in Sabrina's mind was the mouth-watering smells permeating the air. She could pick out garlic, oregano, and basil. She thought she could also detect the telltale scent of very ripe tomatoes grown on a vine instead of those ghastly gas-injected varieties.

A bored waiter approached their table and surprised Sabrina. He had hipster written all over his demeanor, right down to his rolled-up jeans and man bun. "What'll you have?"

"Do you trust me?" Joey asked.

"Sure, but if you order one with everything or anything remotely resembling a meat lover's special, I might offend you when I pick off the pepperonis and sausage."

"Don't worry, this one doesn't have meat. We'll take a large Vongole." Joey turned to Sabrina. "Clams are okay, right?"

"Um, yeah," Sabrina answered.

"Anything to drink?" the waiter asked with a bored expression.

"How about a glass of white wine? The house wine is fine with me," Sabrina answered.

"Same for me," Joey added.

The waiter scribbled on his notepad and strolled away without saying another word.

"I know it's a little dark in here, and the service isn't very good, but I swear it has the best pizza in Seattle," Joey exclaimed.

"I always wonder when people make those sweeping claims. How do you know this? Have you literally had a pizza at every single restaurant in Seattle that serves that popular item? Or did you read that somewhere and take it as fact? I suppose you believe everything you read."

"So cynical for someone so young. No, I don't believe everything I read. I don't believe what I'm learning about in medical school today will be true in a few years. New research will emerge that contradicts half of what the professors are teaching us right now."

"Now who's the cynic?"

Joey adopted a serious expression. "No, not cynical. I believe in lifelong learning. I always want to have someone challenge my beliefs. The minute I stubbornly lock onto something and refuse to entertain another perspective is the day you should throw me off a cliff. People change. People grow. The key to a successful relationship, in my humble opinion, is a healthy amount of disagreement on every little thing. Agreement on the big things, sure. But I shouldn't take the major stuff for granted without thorough exploration. Oh, and growing together, not apart. Never allow yourself to get too cozy or too comfortable. That old pair of shoes might feel good, but eventually old shoes fall apart."

The waiter interrupted them as he set down the two full glasses of wine. At least they weren't miserly with their pours. Sabrina was thankful for that. She was still a little nervous around Joey since she was not at all what Sabrina expected.

"You're quite the surprise, Joey. I don't even know your last name. I think I should know your last name after folding some of your intimate apparel."

"Hartford. Josephine Meredith Hartford. Now you know why I go by Joey. I don't play silly games like not wanting to reveal my middle name. I'm an open book to those I'd like to get to know better. You can ask me anything and I will answer you with complete honesty."

"No person can answer with complete and unadulterated honesty."

Joey scrunched her nose. "Cynic. And your last name?"

"Maxwell," Sabrina answered quickly then moved on to the more interesting part of the conversation. "What I mean is, most of the time, we can't see certain parts of ourselves. Have you ever heard of Johari's window?"

Joey's eyes lit up. "Yes, I have as a matter of fact. Four panes in the window. There's the part of myself I freely share with others and understand about myself. There's the part of myself I know, but don't share with others. With people I grow to love, I'm just gonna tell you, that pane is tiny."

"Good to know. Do you remember the other two panes?"

"Uh huh. Those are the most fascinating. The part of myself that others can decipher, but I don't recognize. That square is my favorite. It fits with my passion for lifelong learning. That pane has the greatest potential for existential growth. I want to learn about what others see; where I can evolve and become a better human being." Joey paused before adding, "The final square is the most compelling. How can there be parts of us that no person can unravel? I can't accept that. I want to have the hope that all mysteries have the potential for uncovering. Otherwise, what is the point?"

"Interesting. I suppose it's about acceptance. Accepting that I cannot control everything, including that some things don't have a neat and tidy answer. Accepting there are ambiguities in the world is freeing. Don't you think?"

"I'll need to ponder that a little while longer. Wow, this conversation took a heavy turn. Can we sneak in a dose of playfulness now?"

"Okay. How old were you when you bought your first pair of boi shorts?"

Joey threw her head back and laughed. "Obsessive much?"

"I'm not the one with twenty-six pairs of underwear. I'm sure I've never owned more than about ten pairs."

"Oh, I have a lot more than twenty-six pairs. Thirteen."

"Thirteen? You have thirteen more pairs?"

"No, I was thirteen. I stole my dad's boxers, and it turned out to be a gateway pair. You know, like a gateway drug. I never went back to boxers after buying my first pair of boi shorts. My turn to ask you a deeply personal question." Joey leaned forward as if she were about to ask a question demanding a break in the protocols on national security.

"Coffee or tea?"

"Definitely coffee," Sabrina answered.

"Well then, you've come to the right city."

The waiter unceremoniously set down the pizza in the middle of the table and Sabrina looked wide eyed at the clams complete with shells sitting on top. She wasn't sure how to eat a piece of pizza that required a person to dig out the meat from a shell.

Joey laughed and served her before placing a piece on her own plate. After methodically plucking out the clams and setting the shells in the empty bowl sitting to the side, she took a large bite. "It's not that hard. You aren't supposed to eat the shells, but you will have to get your hands a little dirty." Joey winked.

"I'm not a priss, you know. I don't mind getting my hands dirty."

The two women ate and made small talk and then Joey set her final piece of pizza down and asked, "Can I ask you something that may or may not be any of my business, but I'm curious?"

"Okay."

"Do you only date women?"

Sabrina nodded. "I know that's rather square of me, isn't it? Being pansexual is all the rage, but I'm not interested in a penis. I'm not that fond of dildos unless they vibrate or are particularly slim. When I was younger, a friend of mine and I went into this sex shop and you know what?"

Joey chuckled. "No, what? I can't imagine what you're going to say. You are very surprising, Sexy Sabrina."

"There was this vibrator with a vibrating jelly tongue. A tongue! Seriously, I'm not making this shit up. The clerk called it the clit kisser. Well, that was it for me. Sold. Although, I briefly entertained the idea of purchasing the alternative Robolick. That one had multiple pink rotating tongues."

Joey bent over and laughed so hard she gulped air as she tried to respond. "Stop. Stop. You're killing me here."

"How about you? I'll bet you're one of those hip, gender fluid, anything goes, types. It's a good thing we'll only be friends. I'd never be able to keep up with you. You probably have men and women lining up outside your apartment door offering an inventive study break and stress reliever."

"You'd be wrong again. One hundred percent lesbian here, but I don't have any negative views of consenting adults making whatever choices meet their needs or desires. I'm not a gold star lesbian or anything. A few years back I had an aha moment as I looked over my intimate experiences. I came to the definitive conclusion that, while I had enjoyed sex with only one man, every single experience with a woman was satisfying. Of course, I needed empirical data to come to that determination. Since medical school, I've done a fair amount of research to cement my conclusions."

"So you've never had a serious relationship?" Sabrina asked.

"I never said that."

"I'm making assumptions again. It sounded like you'd had a lot of different intimate experiences which led me to presume all your relationships were casual."

"Before I started medical school, I was devoted to this woman. We were together for two years. It didn't work out."

"Trust issues?"

"Wrong again. I'm surprisingly trusting for a person who was dumped for another woman. Hell, for a person studying to become a shrink, you misjudge a lot."

"Yeah, I know. I'm much better with people I don't intend to get to know on a more personal level because I can keep that professional distance. Picking up on all the nuances is easy when I'm not involved. I suppose it's like how a person can't participate in a meeting and take minutes at the same time."

"You want to get to know me better?" Joey grinned.

"I suppose the evening hasn't been horrible, but I was serious about strictly friends. And I don't do friends with benefits. I can't separate the intimate act from deeper feelings. Having sex is not only a physical act that feels good. The minute I begin to think like that, my mind considers off-the-wall disgusting things."

"Such as?" Joey asked.

"You're going to wonder why you ever wanted to have dinner with me if I admit this."

"Go for it." Joey gestured with her hand for Sabrina to continue.

"Maybe you'll understand since you're an almost doctor. I start thinking about other bodily functions, like my morning trip to the bathroom after coffee." Sabrina held up her hand. "Hang on, I'll connect the dots. See, my daily business is a kind of release of sorts. If I put sex in the same category, it makes me think too much of my morning crap. Nope, I can't relegate that kind of intimacy to a mere physical sensation."

"You are warped. I like it. What will we have to talk about when we're old and gray? We've already broached the topic of bowel movements. That's a subject the older generation seems so fond of."

Sabrina laughed. "So true. You should have heard my grandmother on regularity. She was a prune pusher when I was in grade school. I hate the damn things to this day. She swore by them. Which was ironic because Mom caught her digging her own shit out of her rectum. She refused to go to the doctor after a nasty bout of constipation."

"You really are a strange one. This is the type of conversation people have with one another after they've known each other for years. That is very dangerous. A compacted bowel can cause complications. And it's extremely painful."

"I know, right?"

"As much as I'd love to continue down this conversational path..."

"You need to return to your jealous lover, right?"

Joey sighed. "Yes, my medical books and journals are waiting for me. I've had such a great time, Sabrina. Honestly. It's been so long since I've had such a wonderful conversation mixed with a healthy dose of laughter. Maybe this is the sort of stress reliever I should pursue versus the alternative. I think I need more empirical data to prove my theory. Will you consider hooking up again?"

"Only if you define hooking up as how we've spent the evening. You know I won't sleep with you tonight, right? The night is almost over."

Joey grabbed Sabrina's hand and squeezed. "I know we're not going to hook up tonight in the more traditional sense of the word and I don't want to."

Sabrina wrinkled her brow. "Should I be offended you don't want to have sex with me? What's wrong with me?"

"Not a single thing, Sexy Sabrina. This has been a perfect evening. I don't want to tarnish it with mind blowing sex." Joey grinned. "Come on, I'll walk you home like the gentlewoman I am." Joey took her hand again and pulled Sabrina to her feet.

"Big sacrifice. We live in the same building." Sabrina bumped Joey who tossed a few bills onto the table before they walked out of the restaurant. "Hey, I was supposed to pay for half."

"You can pay next time."

†

Joey stood in front of 5H and it surprised her that she didn't want to con her way inside the apartment. Sure, she had a lot more studying to complete before she felt good about her progress. But that wasn't the reason. She'd be content with a warm hug from Sabrina. She was honest when she'd said the evening was perfect the way they'd left it after finishing their meal. Looking at Sabrina and the fondness she telegraphed with her eyes, Joey suspected that if she wanted to kiss Sabrina, a slap across her face would not be the response. Joey did not have the time to devote to a relationship and Sabrina was someone worthy of her full attention.

"I'm not going to kiss you, although I kind of want to and I think you do too. If I kiss you, I'll want more, so a hug is all I'll ask for. Friends hug, don't they?"

A sad smile appeared on Sabrina's face. "Yes, friends hug." Sabrina reached around Joey's waist and Joey responded with her own arms pulling Sabrina's body close to hers.

Breathing in Sabrina's fresh clean scent, Joey held on for a long time. She was sure it wasn't more than a minute. A minute was a long time in hugging land. Hugs only lasted a few seconds. Joey released her hold on Sabrina.

"Can I call you if I have free time between study sessions and clinical rotations?"

"You don't have my number. Remember, you got worried I might steal a pair of panties and came down to the laundry room before I could text you."

"Text me tonight after you re-enter your cave. Then I'll have your number," Joey said.

"Okay. Study hard, Joey. I had a wonderful time tonight. I thought you should know that."

Sabrina kissed Joey's cheek, and then Sabrina was gone, leaving an empty feeling. Joey walked back to her apartment and hadn't realized there was another person in the hallway.

"Oh, that's about the sweetest thing I think I've ever seen. My tooth is killing me now. Seriously? What the hell, Joey? You're losing your touch. A kiss on the cheek and a text. She's definitely fuckable. Do you need me to take off the edge so you aren't left hanging?" Maribel made her way down the hallway swaying seductively until she entered Joey's personal space.

"For your information, I don't want to fuck her. We are friends without benefits. There is such a thing as that. Not that it's any of your business. I have a shit ton of studying to do, so no, I'll pass. I'm feeling rather calm right now and don't need to release any pressure. There are plenty of other women who would love to take you up on that offer, go bother them." Joey removed Maribel's hand from where she was making lazy circles on her collarbone.

"Well, if you don't want to fuck her, maybe I'll pay her a visit."

"Don't, Maribel. Leave her alone. She isn't your type."

"Sure she is. She's cute and I sense a kind of hidden passion. It's the quiet ones that are the wildest in bed, you know."

"Whatever. She'll see through your games in a second. I really have to go now." Joey felt the buzz of her phone in her front pocket. She resisted the urge to check fearing it would be Sabrina and then Maribel would attempt to grab her phone and read the message. She hurried down the hall to her apartment. Before Maribel could worm her way inside, she closed the door without chancing a glance at Maribel.

She rested her head against her door praying Maribel would leave. When no knock came, she pulled the phone from her pocket and read the text.

Study hard, then sweet dreams. Thanks for tonight. You better keep your promise to let me buy the sustenance next. Let me know when you pop your head up again.

Joey smiled and thumbed a quick response.

It's a date. How about breakfast tomorrow? It is the most important meal of the day. Or brunch? In case you have church or something.

No church. 9:00 too early?

Nope. See you in 12 hours. Joey was glad Sabrina was not the emoji type because she wasn't either. Occasionally they fit, but not tonight. It took far too much effort to pick out the perfect emojis, and she wanted everything to be perfect when it came to Sabrina. Damn, her final year of medical school was going to be a total bitch in more ways than one.

I'll come get you and be the gentlewoman tomorrow. 5C, right?

Correct.

CHAPTER THREE

Sabrina was still smiling when she heard the crisp knock on her door. Flinging open the door, she expected to find Joey on the other side. *Uh oh.* The last thing Sabrina wanted to do was spend any time with Maribel who had an undercurrent of danger lurking beneath her carefully composed smile. A random thought invaded her mind as she considered how Johari's window ignored those parts of ourselves we present to others that are more fake than real. Maribel was doing it right now. Fake friendliness was the name of the game tonight. Sabrina guessed that if Maribel released her true nature, she'd scratch Sabrina's eyes out and then feed them to her pet snake for good measure.

"Maribel. It's kind of late for a visit."

"Nine isn't late at all. In fact, that's when the night gets interesting. I came by to see if you want to get a drink with me. My treat."

"Actually, I was about to do more work on my dissertation."

Maribel stuck out her lip. "Why are all the beautiful women so focused on their studies? Such a bore and a waste. Come on, I saw you could spare a few hours for Joey. Don't I rate a little time to get to know you better? We're not the only lesbians in the building, but all the others are practically married or butt ugly."

"That is a horrible thing to say." Sabrina weighed her options. Maybe if she capitulated and went for one drink with Maribel, she would avoid a whole host of problems later. Problems she was sure placed Joey smack dab in the center. She could convince Maribel she had no intention of getting in the middle of whatever was happening between the two of them. Even if it was only casual. "One drink, and then I really have to make progress on my neglected dissertation."

"Wonderful. I know just the place." Maribel grabbed Sabrina's hand and pulled her along, barely allowing Sabrina to lock up. "We'll take an Uber, that way we can get hammered and not worry. See I can be responsible."

"Maribel, I said one drink. Why can't we go somewhere close? That's why I moved to Capitol Hill. I wanted to be within walking distance of most everything and a bus ride away to the UW whenever I need to meet with my professor."

"Aw, come on, this place is the bomb. And they make the best mixed drinks in Seattle. Live a little."

"Seriously, one drink and then I'm calling an Uber whether or not you're ready to leave."

"Fine," Maribel agreed.

Before she knew it, a compact car was careening around the corner and pulling up to the entrance of the apartment complex. Both women crawled into the back and settled in for the short ride to the bar Maribel had picked out—a trendy spot that had a mix of gay and straight twenty-somethings grooving to the loud disco-like music. Sabrina fondly remembered her mother playing the seventies-style disco. She had always groaned when her mother had danced around, teasing her father into joining her. Her mother had done this in front of her friends who weren't appalled at all with her mother's flamboyant display.

Sabrina would be lucky if she didn't end up with a massive headache at the end of this evening which had started out so promising. She was second guessing her decision to accept that drink offer from Maribel.

"Hey, why don't I get us the drinks while you see if you can find us a table," Maribel suggested. "What's your poison?"

"Um, anything on the sweet side with rum will be great."

"You got it." Maribel made a beeline for the bar while Sabrina stood by the dance floor, looking around for an empty table. When she saw nothing open, she headed back to the bar noticing two vacant stools near where Maribel was reaching for the drinks. Something caught her attention on the dance floor and when she turned back around, she saw Maribel stirring one of the drinks. Sabrina mimed grabbing the empty stools and Maribel grinned her response holding up the drinks and making her way to where Sabrina was pointing.

After she sat on the tall stool, Sabrina took a sip of the specialty rum drink she'd ordered and thought if this was the best that Seattle had to offer, she would pass the next time around. She rarely imbibed in bitter tasting drinks or something that left an aftertaste. She couldn't put her finger on it, but something tasted off about this drink. Maybe they'd used rotten fruit, but wasn't that what alcohol was, fermented fruit? She hadn't ordered a margarita, so why did the drink taste like there was salt on the rim. Just a hint of saltiness.

Maribel had her fake smile plastered on her face and something about her expression caused alarm bells in Sabrina. Maribel was watching her too closely.

"Drink up, Sabrina, and then we have to dance at least once. One drink, one dance. That's not too much to ask for."

Sweat formed on Sabrina's brow and she gulped down more of her drink although it was too bitter for her taste. The pounding music and alternating lights were causing Sabrina's head to spin. Something wasn't right. She wasn't right. Maybe she was having a reaction to something she'd eaten at dinner. "I...I...don't feel so good. Will you excuse me, please?"

Wobbling, Sabrina headed toward where she thought the bathrooms might be. She felt herself sway, but was determined to make it to one of the stalls in case she needed to throw up. She wasn't sure how she ended up on the floor with her head resting on the cold porcelain and someone trying to rouse her. A cool hand and fingers pressed against her wrist. Sabrina was trying to focus on that voice. A calm, soothing voice. "Sabrina, honey, come on, open those beautiful eyes for me... Fuck, I'm calling 911 and I swear, Maribel, if anything happens to her...."

†

Joey was ignoring the incessant buzzing of her phone. She recognized the number and had no intention of answering the call. She'd considered herself lucky earlier when she'd escaped Maribel's obvious attempt at seduction or a twisted form of blackmail. When she referred to visiting Sabrina, the hairs on the back of Joey's neck had stood at attention.

"Dammit." She picked up the phone, intending to remove it from the vicinity of her books. Out of sight, out of mind. Failing to resist the temptation, she looked at the over thirty text messages. Sabrina's name was like a neon light. Sabrina was in trouble. Real trouble, and Maribel was uncharacteristically panicked. The word *unresponsive* glared at her. Mocking her resolve to stay out of Maribel's drama, *unresponsive* and *Sabrina* in the same sentence sent a sense of dread into Joey's heart.

Grabbing her jacket, she ran out the door, accessing her Uber app to arrange for quick transportation. As she walked and thumbed her request, she took the next minute to text Maribel and instruct her to dial 911 and give the dispatcher detailed information on what was happening and the exact location in the bar. She probably wouldn't be there by the time Joey arrived, but at least she could talk to Maribel and receive an update.

Joey was glad she lived in a popular area of Seattle. Flagging an Uber was always quick because they were so abundant now. R-Place wasn't far, but that didn't stop Joey from wiping her hands on her jeans during the entire ride to the bar. When the car reached the destination she'd given the driver, she reached into her pocket and pulled out a couple of bills to pay the fee.

The lights in the crowded bar irritated an already panicked Joey as she looked around. She saw a mutual acquaintance and fired off a hasty question, "Hey, Shawn, where's Maribel?"

"I think she might still be in the bathroom with that drunk chick she came in with. Man, she looked really out of it. I don't remember seeing either one of them resurface. She's probably fucking her in one of the stalls."

"Thanks, Shawn." Joey rushed to the bathroom, maneuvering around the men and women gyrating on the dance floor to the pounding bass.

Seeing Sabrina on the floor, pasty white with shallow breaths, Joey barked, "Why aren't the paramedics here?"

"I didn't call. Um, I didn't want them asking questions. I could get in real trouble here."

"Maribel, what did you do?"

"I didn't think this would happen. I'm so sorry, Joey, I never intended—"

"Move." Joey squatted next to Sabrina and took her wrist. "Sabrina, Sabrina, it's Joey. Sabrina, come on, open those beautiful eyes for me." Moving a lock of hair, Joey swore through gritted teeth, "Fuck, I'm calling 911, and I swear Maribel if anything happens to her, I will personally see to it that they lock you up and throw away the key. You better hope there's some kind dyke to take care of you while you serve out your sentence. What did you give her?"

"I only thought she might enjoy a little loosening up. Some guy had a little of that date rape drug. He swore it only made them a little less uptight. I didn't plan for this to happen. Maybe I should have expected it since she is a tiny little thing. I probably added too much. Honestly, I didn't believe anything bad would happen. I'm a lot of things, but I wouldn't intentionally harm someone."

"Which one for fuck's sake?"

Maribel shrugged. "I don't know. I didn't ask for the chemical composition or anything."

Joey was wasting time. She pulled out her phone and called. "Please send an ambulance to R-Place on Pine Street. There's a female in her mid-twenties, shallow breaths. Probably drug reaction. I don't know if she's vomited. She is not responsive to her name. Her drink was spiked with something, but I don't know specifically what the drug was. It could have been Ketamine or GHB... Yes, I'll stay with her... No, that's all I know... Thanks, yes if anything changes, I'll let you know... Yes, I know CPR."

Joey placed her finger on Sabrina's neck, fearing her condition would worsen before the paramedics arrived. Her night was officially shot. Joey wouldn't return to her studies or rest until she was sure Sabrina was out of danger. Suddenly, Sabrina's weak pulse was hard to find. Joey carefully laid her on the floor and began CPR seconds before the Paramedics arrived and took over. They seemed to find a pulse and at least that was a relief to Joey. Working as a team, the efficient medical professionals had Sabrina on a gurney, wheeling her away. The tube they'd pushed in her throat was not a good sign, but Joey had seen her fair share of drug overdoses come away from the experience relatively unaffected. Sabrina looked healthy. Definitely fit. She would be okay.

"What hospital?" Joey called out.

"Harborview," the woman answered with a pitying smile. The attractive female paramedic probably thought Sabrina was Joey's girlfriend. *I wish.*

"Um, can I come with?" Maribel asked. "I want to make sure she's okay. Apologize or something. Maybe see if there's anything I can do to make it up to her. I know I fucked up. I'm really sorry."

"I don't think that's a good idea, Maribel. If she sees you and you confess, you could get in a lot of trouble."

"You would lie for me?"

"No, I won't lie for you, but I won't offer any information. I'll be there for her when she wakes up. She'll be confused and scared. I think a friendly face is important. I don't know if she has any family or close friends nearby. We didn't talk much about that..."

"Okay. Text me later to let me know how she's doing." Maribel walked away. Her shoulders drooped and Joey got the sense that underneath it all was a decent human being trying to emerge. But only if Maribel lost that underlying malady. The one that caused her to make terrible decisions and obsess in an unhealthy manner about women who were unobtainable.

CHAPTER FOUR

Sabrina's pounding head forced her to open her eyes. The room was bright and her throat felt like when she'd had strep as a teenager. She looked down at her arm and saw an IV hooked up and then she noticed another person sitting in a chair about ten feet away. "What...what happened?"

Joey cautiously approached the bed. She concentrated on measuring her response. "Maribel called me last night when you went into the bathroom and she couldn't rouse you."

"I remember feeling sick. I only agreed to one drink, and I never get drunk. I don't understand. Do you think it was something I ate? Can something like this happen to people who get salmonella?"

Joey perched on the side of the bed and stroked Sabrina's head. "No. I'm sure it wasn't food poisoning or related to our dinner. Your throat is a little raw because of the tube. Airways are funny. They need to stay open all the time. I know it's inconvenient to breathe twenty-four seven, but it's kind of essential to life."

"My head is killing me."

Joey leaned in and kissed Sabrina's forehead. "I'll get a nurse. Stay put. Okay? No running marathons or whatever you do to keep that fine ass of yours looking so good."

A weak chuckle escaped from Sabrina's lips. Joey brushed her fingers down Sabrina's arm before standing and exiting the room. Sabrina turned her head to the right, looking for the pitcher of water that always seemed to reside on a rolling nightstand. Her lips felt chapped, and she was dying of thirst. Pushing with her hands she attempted to maneuver her body to a semi-sitting position. Feeling along the edge of the bed, she searched for the buttons to help adjust her position.

A smiling nurse walked into the room as Joey trailed behind. "I hear you might need something for your head. On a scale of one to ten, how much pain are you experiencing right now?"

"Um...about a six, I guess. Can you help me find the button? I'd like to sit up and maybe drink a little water, please."

"Sure, let me get that for you." The nurse pressed a button and the head of the bed rose bit by bit.

The hum of the motor was surprisingly quiet, and she was grateful for that. Any amount of noise caused her head to throb. Maybe she'd under-reported the level of pain she was experiencing.

"Thanks. Um, can I revise that number? I think an eight might be closer to the truth."

"All right. I'll talk to the doctor and bring you something in a minute." The nurse grabbed the water with a plastic straw sticking out and handed it to Sabrina. "Can I get you anything else?"

"Yeah. Discharge papers."

"We'll see what the doctor says. He might agree to it after he checks you out. You have someone who can stay with you today, right?"

"I didn't do this to myself, if that's what you think. It's frustrating because I don't remember a lot. If it wasn't food poisoning..." Sabrina caught Joey's eyes before she quickly looked away. There was definitely something Joey wasn't telling her. She saw guilt. She knew that look. Joey had quickly averted her eyes, and that wasn't like Joey at all. She never had a problem maintaining eye contact. "Spill it, Joey. What aren't you telling me?"

"Your drink was spiked," Joey mumbled.

"I'll get those meds and let the doctor know you don't need a psyche evaluation."

"No, I don't need an evaluation or placement on a suicide watch. Thanks."

After the nurse left, Sabrina focused on Joey. She was still trying to unravel what had happened to her. "I don't understand. I wasn't on a date. Why would someone spike my drink? I don't remember talking to any strange men. Did a guy approach me? It was a gay bar. That doesn't make sense."

"No, it wasn't a man."

"Maribel?"

"I don't think she meant for this to happen."

"Are you defending her?"

"No, of course not, but I know for a fact she feels terrible about what happened and I don't think pressing charges will do any good for anyone."

Sabrina laid her head back. "No, I don't suppose it would. At some point, Maribel will have to accept responsibility for whatever poor decisions she makes. I won't be the one to push her further. But, Joey, I think Maribel needs a little help. One of these days her reckless behavior will cause an outcome she can't fix with an apology or sincere regret."

"She isn't a complete shit. She has a good side."

"I know. We all have our issues and few people are without redemption. I'll have to work hard to see her positive qualities after the stunt she pulled on me, but I'll try." Sabrina closed her eyes. She was still trying to fend off the effect of the drug. But if she gave in to her drowsiness, they might not let her leave. When she opened her eyes again, a welcoming sight did not appear before her.

†

It took every ounce of restraint on Joey's part to resist striking out at Maribel as she entered the hospital room. A bouquet hid her face. Joey guessed the peace offering was an attempt to mask her sheepishness at her foolish action of the previous evening. Coming undone and letting Maribel have it in front of Sabrina wouldn't do anyone any good right now as she'd expressed earlier.

"Hey," Maribel began. "How are you feeling? Look, I'm really sorry..."

Joey squinted at Maribel, evaluating her apology. It seemed sincere. But was she apologizing because she was afraid Joey and Sabrina would blow the whistle on her, or was she truly sorry? It was hard to tell with Maribel. Joey was sure of one thing and one thing only. She was done with Maribel. She didn't want anything to do with her after today. No more late-night fuck sessions. The friend part of the friends with benefits was a stretch. She wasn't friends with Maribel. She was more like an acquaintance, a conveniently warm body.

Sabrina shifted in bed. "What you did was reckless and dangerous, but I'm not going to press charges if that's what you're worried about. I will, however, suggest that you see a friend of mine—"

Maribel's eyes took on that dangerous glint that gave Joey the creeps. "Fuck you and your psychobabble pals. I don't need a fucking shrink. Been there, done that. I believe he fucked me up more than before I saw that creep. You know, your profession has a lot of sickos in it. How about practicing those skills on each other because goddess knows every last one of you needs a serious head shrinking?"

"I promise, she's good. I don't know about your experiences. Clearly, they weren't positive, but I think you'd like—"

Maribel flung the flowers on the bed cutting Sabrina off. "Forget it, see ya around, do-gooder." Stalking out of the room, she turned her head and tossed a parting comment to Joey. "Give me a call when you get bored, lover."

Joey felt Sabrina's intense scrutiny and turned to capture her eyes. "I know, you don't need to warn me."

"I'm not your mother or your lover, I wasn't about to say anything. Besides, you're an intelligent woman, my assessment of the situation isn't anything you don't already know."

Joey grinned. "Assessment of the situation. That's so…clinical. Maybe I'd like your professional assessment of me."

"I don't want to be your therapist, either."

"What do you want, Sabrina?"

"Definitely not what you've offered."

"Yes, you've made that abundantly clear, but that's not the question I asked. I already know what you don't want, answer the question. Geez, you sound more like a lawyer in training."

"I don't know yet. That is honestly my answer."

"I have a proposal."

"Intriguing."

"You're in your final year of school, right?"

Sabrina nodded.

"How about we become study buddies? Sometimes I need a break and it would be nice to, well, you know, take those breaks with—"

"I'm not going to be your study fuck buddy—"

"No, no, that wasn't what I meant to suggest. I…um…I like talking with you. How about we use our breaks to explore the deep dark secrets of the universe? If I hadn't chosen the medical profession, I would have studied philosophy. There aren't too many people interested in having deep and meaningful discussions. It's refreshing. I think it might help me focus."

"Okay," Sabrina agreed without an argument.

"Okay? That's it? That's your response?"

"Did you want me to couch my affirmative answer within some deeper philosophical context? Perhaps a witty analogy?"

Joey threw her head back and laughed. "How about I use my considerable charm to get you out of here? Maybe you'll be so grateful, you'll—"

"Stop. I'll be grateful, but that is where it ends. You can't help yourself, can you?" Sabrina chuckled.

"Nope." Joey stood and winked at Sabrina before leaving to find the nurse who held the keys to Sabrina's release from the hospital.

CHAPTER FIVE

Uber was the best way to get around in Seattle. Parking was always a huge challenge. Yet, there was something inherently wrong about arriving back at the apartment complex in an Uber. Sabrina was glad for the company on her trip back. Secretly, she wished Joey had a car to bring her back home versus what amounted to a modern-day cab. Beggars couldn't be choosy though. She couldn't help herself, she had to ask.

"You don't have a car?"

"Nope. I have a bike, but I didn't think you wanted me to take you home on a bike."

"Oh, I don't know, a motorcycle ride might have been fun." Sabrina smiled at Joey. "I don't have anything fancy, but you can always use my car. Although in Seattle I think it's more of a hassle than it's worth to drive anywhere."

Joey retrieved a bill from her wallet. "Thanks, that's nice of you to offer. I'll keep that in mind if I ever need one. And regarding the bike, I meant human powered. A bicycle."

"Hey, let me get this. I don't expect you to pay for my return trip from the hospital. It was nice of you to hang around until they sprung me. It's the least I can do. I'll bet you're stressed about all the study time you've lost."

Joey shrugged. "Okay, I don't have any hang-ups over who pays. Your place or mine?"

"Huh?" Joey's question perplexed Sabrina.

"I have a shit ton of studying to catch up on and I presume you do as well. We negotiated a study buddy system, right? Or, was I hallucinating our conversation this morning?"

"Oh, right. Depends. I think we need to determine who has the best snacks."

"Well, I am in medical school, so my snacks might not be the ones most people gravitate to, but they are healthier and the far better choice."

"You're making assumptions, Joey. What kind of snacks do you think I have?"

"Ice cream, candy, potato chips...you know, the absolute last choice for brain food."

"Okay, you win. Yeah, I stock up on junk food. I'm a stress eater. I admit that. I suppose you have only fresh vegetables and whole foods with that six-pack of yours. Figures."

"I have plenty of protein because carbs are death to my need for study stamina and the full use of my brain. After you cleanse your system, you will grow to crave healthy foods. I promise, you won't miss all that crap you've been putting in your body. And, bonus, you'll have an amazing clarity of thought. You'll realize what a catch I am and decide—"

Sabrina backhanded Joey. "Fine, your place, and I'll eat your crappy health food."

Joey shook her head. "I've developed this mix of fruit, nuts, seeds, and chocolate—dark chocolate. I promise you're going to love it and every item is a proven brain food. Delicious, nutritious, and perfect for studying. If you don't love it and it doesn't satisfy your craving, go ahead and run to your apartment to retrieve whatever fistful of empty calorie carbo toxin you wish to poison your body with. Be my guest, but don't blame me when you're forty and diabetes comes knocking at your door."

Sabrina chuckled. "You had me at chocolate."

†

Concentrating on her studies was proving harder than Joey thought. She'd reread the same paragraph four times now. Sabrina was staring off into space and Joey was dying to ask her what she was thinking about. She'd stopped typing on her laptop several minutes ago and had a kind of pained expression on her face. If Joey had to label the look, it wouldn't fit into a neat box. Pained wasn't the right word. Joey thought she looked like she was trying to figure out a complex math problem and the answer was just out of reach.

Joey watched as Sabrina kept tapping her index finger on her lips. Her luscious, kissable lips. Joey was only human, and that would distract anyone.

"Okay, tell me. What's causing that tiny wrinkle in your forehead and the tap, tap, tapping on your gorgeous lips?"

"Huh?" Sabrina's eyes rested casually on Joey's. "What are you babbling about?"

"I want to take a short break and ask about your work and the problem that seems to have caused so much consternation."

"Oh, that? I was thinking about our conversation the other night and then Maribel came over and that got me thinking about someone else."

"I'm not sure I like the direction this might be going. Maribel shouldn't be in your thoughts at all and if she is, nothing good can come of it." Joey frowned.

"I wasn't thinking of the spiked drink or my unplanned visit to Harborview. I was thinking about my dissertation and if it would be worth it to trash a half a year's work to expand on Johari's window."

"Now, you've got my interest piqued, but can you afford to switch gears this late in the game?" Joey asked.

"I know, that was what I was contemplating. It's painful to even consider switching topics at this late stage. On the other hand, I don't care for the one I've chosen. My professors talked me into it."

"What's the topic?"

"False memories," Sabrina answered.

"Sounds interesting."

"Oh, it is. It's fascinating, really, but still not something I'm all that passionate about—other than reading and maybe writing a short paper on it."

"So how were you going to expand on Johari's window and what would you need to do to convince your professors?"

Excitement shone in Sabrina's eyes. "Do you seriously want to hear about it?"

"I do," Joey said with conviction.

"I thought Johari might have missed a major piece with his window, but that would change the window to something else because nobody has ever seen a five paned window."

"Stained glass windows can have a lot more than four panes," Joey offered.

Sabrina nodded. "True. Don't you think most of us, whether conscious or unconscious, present a side of ourselves that isn't real? A facade. That seems to happen a lot when a person is first dating and wants to put their best foot forward. That's conscious, but where does that fit into Johari's window, and is there a way to determine if this facade is conscious?"

Joey grabbed her chin and nodded. "Interesting. Yeah, I suppose you're right. But, even when we put our best foot forward, isn't that still a part of who we are?"

"I don't think so. It's not that we always want to lie to ourselves or others, we're simply unreliable witnesses. Take Maribel. I think she is not at all who she presents to the outside world and I'm not sure she recognizes that about herself."

"So why doesn't that fall into the quadrant of either not known to her or others or not known to her, but known to others."

Sabrina jumped up and paced. "Because that facade could be in any of the squares. I could try to show my best side to you and you see it. That's the known to myself and known to others square. Or maybe my best side isn't me at all and I'm hiding behind the facade, so it's known to me, but not known to you because I'm superb at faking it. Do you see what I'm saying?"

"Kind of. What about those people who are, 'what you see is what you get'?"

"They don't exist."

Joey raised her eyebrow. "I never try to put my best foot forward. I am what I am. That's what gets me in trouble sometimes."

"Bullshit. I call bullshit. You agonized over what to wear for dinner. I'll bet you a free pass to unhealthy snacks you changed at least once before settling on that sexy button-down shirt and tight black pants."

"They were not tight."

"Maybe not, but they sure hugged your body and fit like a glove. Nice diversion from admitting that I was right."

"Okay fine. I accede to your advanced observational skills." Joey waggled her eyebrows. "So...you liked my choice. Enough to—"

"Perhaps a little facade would work to your advantage, Ms. I-am-what-I-am."

"Touché. I'm too honest. Others say I'm far too blunt and that is not an attractive trait. I should work on that. I really should. You're right about that being a handy skill when talking with patients. I'd read that dissertation, which is saying a lot. Aren't most of them boring?"

"Not really. I find social psychology fascinating. People are interesting, don't you think?"

"I suppose so. I prefer the hard sciences. Much easier to decipher what the data is telling you. Order a test and the results come back. That helps us decide on next steps. Trying to figure out people, specifically women who are masters at facade, is something I've never been good at." Joey stretched her body and stood. "Can I ask you something?"

"Sure."

"What do you see when you look at me? You know, the pane where other people see something I can't see myself. And is that different from this fifth pane you're talking about? What's my fake self?" Joey asked.

Sabrina looked toward the ceiling, then met Joey's eyes. "Hmm, that's a good question. I suppose, a person's fake self is easier to spot when you first meet someone, but you aren't sure if that's the real person. Okay, first impression?"

"Yeah, I guess your first impression is a good place to start."

"You want me to be totally honest?"

"No, I want you to lie and make me feel good." Joey laughed. "Of course I want you to be honest."

"Okay. You come off as this cool, confident person, who has their whole life planned and everything is coming together perfectly. No attachments or roadblocks allowed as you pursue your path in life. You want people to believe you don't care one whit what they think of you."

"But..."

"But I think you care. At least you care about what some people think."

"I care what you think," Joey said.

"I know."

†

"Food. I need real food, not snacks," Sabrina complained.

"Well, we have been at it for six hours. Have you decided to make life miserable by starting over on your dissertation?"

Sabrina frowned and looked dejected. "No, as appealing as my idea to create a stained-glass window to replace Johari, I can't bring myself to throw five months of dedicated work out the window. Pun completely unintended."

Joey clapped her hands together. "Perfect. Then we can spare a few hours to get a bit of fresh air and have an early dinner. A *lunner* or *dinch*."

"What did you say?"

"Oh, sorry. Sometimes I smoosh words together to make a new one. My mom used to do that. It always brought me out of whatever foul mood I was in. I was a brooding teen. She had the magic touch. That's one of the first things that drew me to you. I loved when you called me Ms. Misorude."

Sabrina smiled. "I can't believe you do that too."

"Seriously, we ought to throw in the towel and get married right now. I think I've met my soul mate," Joey joked. "Who else on this planet does that?"

"No one I know of. We can't get married, though. You're moving to some backwater place to tend to the rural needs of the underserved and I need to be a part of civilization. No theater, fine food and wine, or concerts makes this little lesbian a very grumpy woman."

Joey waggled her eyebrows. "You know, entertainment comes in many forms. Happy couples make their own entertainment. There are always books and web TV."

"Not the same. I grew up in a small town and I swore I would never go back to a place with small-minded people who can't keep their big fat noses out of my business." Sabrina leaned back and crossed her ankles.

"I'm gonna make it my mission to change your mind about small towns. What are you doing next weekend?"

Sabrina shrugged. "Until I finish my dissertation, you are looking at it. Besides taking shifts at the clinic, I spend most of my free hours, writing and rewriting this blasted document. Oh, and meeting with my professors who critique every stage, adding numerous hours of research to my already hefty mountain of work."

"Come with me to check out Forks."

"Doesn't it rain all the time there?"

Joey blew a raspberry. "Pfft. Not any more than Seattle. That's what the HR person said."

"You know you can't trust a recruiter. They lie. Besides, isn't Forks where all those vampires are?"

Joey bent over and laughed uproariously. "A *Twilight* fan, really? Who are you?"

Sabrina mock glared at Joey. "I see you know all about *Twilight*. So, who is the fan here?"

"Come on. We can go see the rain forest and take the gold star *Twilight* tour?"

"Is that really a thing?" Sabrina asked.

"Maybe," Joey hedged. "Okay, I'm not sure what they call it, but there is a tour and a big celebration each year for Bella's birthday."

"Ah ha, you are a rabid *Twilight* follower. I knew it." Sabrina set her laptop on the floor and emerged from the chair she'd molded her body to for the past six hours between periodic visits to the bathroom. She shoved Joey. "Okay, I'll go with you. I have always wanted to see the rain forest. Plus, I keep holding out for Alice realizing she's a lesbian or, at the very least, fluid."

"Not on team Bella? Huh? Well, I'm partial to Rosalie. I kind of like the bad girl types. She was far more interesting. And, you have to admit, Bella was a little irritating. Pasty white, whiny baby who can't decide between Edward or Jacob. Neither of which appealed to me."

"Well, duh, that's because you're a lesbian." Sabrina chuckled. "I cannot believe we are talking about *Twilight*. I should be very embarrassed to know as much as I do about the series. I'm only slightly less appalled knowing you are as well versed as I am with the characters."

Joey looped her arm inside Sabrina's. "Let's do dinch, darling," she said in what Sabrina assumed was her best posh accent. "I have another great place to take you to and we can explore the pros and cons of bedding each *Twilight* character. We can plan our big trip to Forks."

"I want paraphernalia for proof I took the gold star tour. If you buy me a trinket, I'll go."

"Wow, you drive a hard bargain. Done, but you're paying for dinch."

"Fine, but I think it is closer to dinner, not lunner or dinch as you so adorably presented."

"I like that, adorably presented. I think I'm wearing you down." Joey led Sabrina out the door.

The tinkle of laughter filled the small apartment and traveled into the hallway as the two women exited for their early dinner.

†

"Well, well, well. Don't you two look cozy?" Maribel was leaning against the wall next to the front entrance of the building. "I see you've bounced back. You must be in stellar physical condition. I didn't take you for a health nut like this one." Maribel pointed to Joey.

"Not that it is any of your business, but we were studying all day and needed to grab something to eat before hitting the books again," Joey said.

Maribel pushed away from the wall. "Great, where are we going?"

Sabrina shifted her gaze to Joey before addressing Maribel. She was looking for the slightest reaction to know how to continue. Joey's pinched look and barely perceptible flinch gave Sabrina all the evidence she needed to proceed. "I'm not sure you would be interested in our dinner conversation. I've been bouncing dissertation ideas off Joey. I think you've made it abundantly clear what you think about mental health professionals. Unless...you'd like to be part of my research studies. I am always looking for additional participants." Sabrina shot Maribel an evil grin.

Maribel looked as if she'd eaten a piece of rotten meat. "No thanks. When you two are done with your snorefest, call me and we can grab a drink." She held up her hands in a placating gesture. "I promise, I would never do a repeat of last night. Just a friendly drink to make it up to you."

"Considering we both lost a lot of valuable time with the fiasco last night, we'll need to regretfully decline your generous offer," Joey interjected. Sabrina noted the bitterness and sarcasm in her tone.

"Hmm, Joey, I didn't take you as a person who holds a grudge. What's the big deal? You'd think you were the one I—"

Joey lunged for Maribel, and Sabrina put out her arm to stop Joey's progress. "Maybe some other time," Sabrina offered. "If we can catch up, I think a night out would do both of us good and we'll for sure take you up on your offer for a drink. How's that?"

"Perfect. Oh, and Joey, you know where to find me if you need another kind of break," Maribel said in a singsong voice before strolling away with a swing to her hips.

"Joey—"

"I know. She's a dangerous person to tangle with. I am very much regretting my friendship with Maribel right about now. You don't have to be a trained professional to recognize how unstable Maribel is. I'm not sure how to establish new boundaries without lighting a powder keg."

"That's a tough one. I think it will be difficult for Maribel to hear she needs help from anyone. Successful conversations with a person who needs help all comes down to motivation. If you want her to seek help because you genuinely care about her, that will give you an advantage. I can help you with that. If you want her to get help for selfish reasons, such as you are done with her antics, honestly, that won't go over so well. She'll sense your insincerity."

Joey nodded. "I'll need to think on that. Do I care enough about Maribel to talk with her is a great question. I suppose that doesn't shed a positive light on me. Here I have this friendship with her—with benefits I might add."

"Yeah, I'm well aware of the nature of your relationship," Sabrina added wryly.

"I feel like a total shit. I thought this was a mutual thing. You know, we were both getting what we wanted and needed. But...now it feels like I kinda took advantage of the situation. I guess I haven't been a stellar friend. I've taken, without giving anything in return."

"Maybe not. I think you care more for Maribel than you realize. Focus on that. It will allow you to have a genuine conversation. You'll have to shed that facade you present to the outside world ninety percent of the time. Dig deep for that caring individual that exists below the surface." Sabrina smiled.

"But it takes so much more energy to drag that boring side out." Joey tugged on Sabrina, causing her to veer to the right.

"It is never boring to show how much you care." Sabrina wondered how much of a loaded statement that really was. She was starting to care for Joey. Far more than she wanted to. It would be so easy to allow their friendship to evolve to something more. But what would that be? Friends with benefits was out of the question. Was there something in between a full-blown committed relationship and occasional fuck buddies who cared for one another?

Joey sighed. "I don't have much time to devote to anything beyond a surface relationship. Caring means time and effort. Remember, I have a very jealous lover who doesn't want me to care about anyone else but her, at least not until I complete medical school."

"You can't control how you feel about someone. I agree maintaining a healthy relationship takes time and effort. Caring about someone is a different kettle of fish." Sabrina was sure the small worry lines between her brows were showing. They always appeared when she had a difficult dilemma to solve. Joey fit the bill, and she could not control her burgeoning feelings. Joey kept making things clear she did not have the capacity for anything along the lines of what Sabrina knew she yearned for. Damn feelings, they were bound to screw up her best laid plans.

"Now there's an interesting saying. Kettle of fish. What the hell does that even mean?" Joey asked.

Sabrina chuckled. "I don't know. We could always Google it."

"Nah, sometimes it is better to leave a few mysteries unsolved."

"You mean like the mystery of how much...oh damn. I said that out loud, didn't I?"

"Unfortunately, you didn't really say a lot. If you're looking for fill in the blank, I think there are several choices." Joey placed her index finger on her gorgeous mouth. "How much you want to rip off my clothes. How about how much you're attracted to me? Or how much you are looking forward to coming to Forks with me? Am I getting hot?"

Yes, yes, yes and yes, Sabrina thought, but instead said, "How much I can fit in my small body once real food gets anywhere near my mouth. I hope we're close because I'm about to consider cannibalism perfectly acceptable."

"Does eating pussy count as cannibalism, because I could—"

"It was a joke," Sabrina clarified.

"You're adorable when you get flustered."

CHAPTER SIX

Joey wondered why they labeled clinical rotations as clerkships. It sounded too much like law school to her, but that was what was on the curriculum for her fourth year. She'd enjoyed the clerkships of the previous year and now she was eager to delve into the Emergency Medicine rotation. She'd nabbed a cherry spot at Harborview. It didn't get any better than that.

Joey knew her fellow medical school classmates did not spend the hours she did after her day ended, but she liked to combine the didactic learning with what she'd experienced during the day. She would often spend hours on research and reading after whatever situation had presented itself during her shift. This didn't leave a lot of time for a social life, but she knew it would pay off when her boards came around and when she interviewed for her residency. Joey hadn't yet decided where she would do her residency, but that didn't matter because she would be more prepared than anyone else in her class. Maintaining a top ranking had always been important to her. Lately, she was wondering how much of life she was missing out on and if her priorities were in the right spot.

With a nervousness uncharacteristic of Joey, she tapped her pen on the table next to her laptop. She wondered what Sabrina was up to tonight. They'd been spending a lot of time together, but Sabrina had been cagey about what she was planning on doing this evening and that unsettled Joey. Her nervousness combined with curiosity over what Sabrina was hiding was almost too much to bear. And Sabrina was definitely hiding something. Was she on a date? Maybe she was a criminal and hiding a life of crime. Joey laughed to herself as she envisioned Sabrina sneaking into her apartment and stealing a pair of her special boi shorts.

"Fuck it," Joey said out loud.

She picked up her cell phone and thumbed a text to Sabrina.

After your secret rendezvous with your lover, wanna get a bite to eat? I need a calming presence before I start my clerkship tomorrow.

Joey kept tapping her pen on the table. The staccato beat increased as her agitation grew. Sabrina always responded right away to her texts. What the hell? She'd acted strange about today—deliberately leaving out what prior engagement she had and with whom. Joey wasn't sure it was a previous engagement, but she'd made assumptions. Maybe those assumptions weren't correct. They'd been spending most of their free time together and had made a habit out of grabbing a bite to eat after studying. Surely a forgotten meeting or commitment would be the only thing taking her away. After the call Sabrina had received earlier, she had tried to sound casual about having to leave and had told Joey she should go get something to eat on her own or call Maribel if she wanted company while taking a break.

Startled from her thoughts by a quick rapping on her door, Joey jumped up to answer. She was hoping Sabrina was back from wherever she'd gone. The smile slipped off her face like molten wax after she opened the door and Maribel smirked at her.

"Hey lover, I thought you might want a break. Since little miss vanilla scooted out of here earlier like she needed to stop the world from a path of self-destruction, I decided you needed me."

Joey didn't make a move to invite Maribel in. She wondered what information Maribel had, and tried to weasel it out of her. "So, did she say where she was going?"

Maribel narrowed her eyes. "Don't you know? I thought you two were besties."

"Stop with the barbs, Maribel. Either you know something or you don't."

"Sorry, if I'd known how important that information was, I would have interrogated her for you. Maybe slipped a truth serum into her drink. I'm good at that."

"Fuck, Maribel, haven't you—"

"I was kidding, you dolt. She seemed distracted and agitated. I figured it was something important. She's usually more polite. Not that I deserve her good manners, but if I didn't know any better, I'd think she grew up in the South. They're like that, you know, all mannered and pleasant on the outside, but watch out. I know what 'bless her heart' really means."

"She's not from the South. Midwest, I think." Joey continued to block the doorway. Her message was clear. She was not about to invite Maribel inside. She didn't need to start up that craziness again.

"Okay, that makes sense. Hey, aren't you going to invite me in? I know you didn't grow up in the Midwest or South, so impeccable manners aren't your thing, but—"

"Nope. I still have work to do and I've already exhausted the time allowed for a break."

Maribel pursed her lips. "I see right through your crap. You were hoping the pasty personality would be back by now."

"Whatever." Joey started to shut the door when Maribel stuck her foot inside to block Joey's attempt to end the conversation.

"One drink. I think you owe me that considering you've ignored me for the last two weeks. I thought we were friends. Or are you that much of an asshole? You know, the type of person that takes what you need without giving anything back in return?"

"I don't recall hearing complaints regarding my ability to contribute. I believe I gave you exactly what you needed. No strings attached. Mind-blowing sex without guilt."

"I think that's my contribution. Not yours."

"Now I call bullshit. I distinctly remember you screaming my name as you came all over my mouth."

Maribel smiled. "Okay, true. Still, you can afford a few minutes for your previous fuck buddy."

Joey opened the door and waved Maribel inside. "Fine, but I don't have time for our usual stress relieving session. One drink. Maybe we can try something different."

"Like?"

"Conversation. I know you aren't as shallow or dim-witted as you'd like people to believe."

"I never said I was stupid. I simply choose to highlight my other skills. I can be a witty conversationalist. How was I supposed to figure out that was something you craved when your stress levels increased to the boiling over point?"

"I'm not stressed so perhaps we can give this a try?"

"All right." Maribel sauntered to the couch and sat. She relaxed back into the cushions and asked, "Do you still have that tasty scotch? If so, I'll take some of that."

Joey filled a tumbler with the amber liquid and grabbed a bottle of water for herself. She handed the scotch to Maribel. "Here."

"You aren't having one?"

"No. Can I ask you something?"

"Ooh, jumping right in, huh? Are we going to get all philosophical before we fuck?"

Joey could feel the anger rise. Why had she thought it was possible to have a serious conversation with Maribel? She opened her mouth to speak but before she had a chance to shut Maribel down, Maribel interrupted.

"Sorry. Old habits. I'll be good. Sure, what do you want to know?"

"Is everyone just a big fake? Hiding behind some version of who they think the world wants to see? And if that's the case, can anyone see through the veneer? You know, get to the real core?"

Maribel seemed to consider Joey's question and her serious expression surprised Joey. She was about to get an unvarnished response from Maribel. Perhaps this would be the only time Maribel would be honest with her. Maybe she'd show a side that wasn't the troubled devious person Joey thought she was, down to her tiniest molecule.

Maribel set her glass on the table. "I think there are parts of ourselves we don't show to anyone, not even ourselves. Yeah, I think most of what people show to the world is a fake outer covering, especially in new relationships. But over time there are those who will worm their way into your heart and soul. Those fortunate individuals get a glimpse into the real person. Each person is different. Some people give up the gloss more quickly than others. I call those people open books. They are like the sluts of intimacy. They'll open up to anyone. Ironically, those are the kind who'll slam their legs shut and won't fuck just anyone. Sexual promiscuity and emotional promiscuity do not go hand in hand."

"What about individuals who are closed to both?"

"They're the saddest of the lot. Complete isolation. That kind are good at hiding everything."

Joey nodded. "It's hard to tell, huh? What's real and what's fake. How do you get to the core then?"

Maribel shrugged. "I don't know. Perseverance. Genuine interest. I'd be flattered if someone cared enough to see the real me. It's never happened. Not really."

Joey studied Maribel. "Maybe if you gave the slightest hint that's what you wanted, they would."

Maribel picked up the scotch from the table and drained her drink. "Boring. If we're not gonna fuck, I'm outta here." She stood and headed for the door.

And the shell is back. "I'm sorry, Maribel. I haven't been a good friend." Joey thought she had briefly turned Maribel over to expose the soft vulnerable side, but then Maribel had righted herself and tucked her head back inside the turtle shell.

Maribel turned and looked at Joey. A sadness crept into her eyes. "No, you've been exactly the kind of friend you said you would be. I knew the score. I accepted the boundaries to the agreement. No sense in changing the rules mid-stream."

†

How in the world had Carolyn sucked Sabrina in again? Carolyn had called out of the blue. She'd moved to Seattle. Wasn't that awesome, she'd said. They should get together, she mentioned—almost as an afterthought. Sabrina knew better. It was a calculated move. There was a lot more to the story. Of that, Sabrina was sure.

The hospital had mentioned Carolyn was on a forty-eight hour hold until they decided whether to admit her to an inpatient facility. The problem was no openings, and they weren't the best choice for her to get the treatment she needed.

"Fuckity, fuck, fuck," Sabrina hissed as she made her way through the Seattle traffic. She should have used Uber again, but she'd wanted to have the security of her own car. She didn't want to wait outside for a ride back to her apartment or, God forbid, have to call Joey for moral support. Joey wouldn't understand why she was rushing off to be there for Carolyn.

Why was Sabrina listed on the form? A person to notify. The loved one to call. The nurse had sounded concerned. Carolyn had given her permission to release every bit of information about her condition. This had been a serious attempt, the nurse had informed Sabrina. There wasn't any hesitancy. It was a miracle she was still alive.

Finding a parking space in the large garage, Sabrina made her way to the room. She kept looking for the signs that would take her to the wing where Carolyn was waiting for her. She knew it was unkind to envision Carolyn perched on the bed like a bird of prey—ready to swoop down on her and gobble her whole. Those talons would sink into her side as she was once again carried away.

After she tenuously pushed open the door, she couldn't control the gasp that erupted from her mouth. Carolyn had never looked so pale. So utterly destroyed. It was as if someone had overtaken her body and used and abused it to the point of breakage. Sabrina's compassion took over as she rushed to the side of the bed and took Carolyn's bandaged arm.

"Sorry. I never meant to live. I thought the worst that would happen is you would make sure someone took care of my remains. Then maybe say a few kind words for old times' sake," Carolyn whispered.

"What about your parents? Do you want me to call and talk with them?"

Even in her compromised physical state the look she gave Sabrina was unmistakable disbelief. Of course that wasn't an option or a remote consideration.

"You're fucking kidding, right?" Carolyn rolled her eyes. "My father would chastise me for not finishing the job. He'd think an unsuccessful suicide attempt was another failure in a long line of fuck-ups."

"Your father's a bastard, but your mom would want to know."

"Don't. She has to put up with enough shit from my father. You know my father always liked you, but then again it was probably because he wanted to fuck you."

Sabrina winced. "Okay, we can talk about this later and perhaps revisit letting your mom know where you are. She deserves at least that because I'm sure you disappeared and she hasn't heard from you in months."

"My life took a bad turn after you left. I'm not blaming you," Carolyn hastened to add.

"What happened?" Sabrina asked softly.

"New addiction took over. It sort of paired well with my old one. But this one is far more destructive."

"Drugs?" Sabrina guessed.

The almost imperceptible head nod broke Sabrina's heart. She loved Carolyn once, and that was something impossible to ignore.

"So, what's the plan after they release you?" Sabrina asked.

Tears formed in Carolyn's eyes. "I don't have a plan. I didn't expect to live."

Shit, shit, shit. Why did Sabrina feel like Carolyn was now her responsibility? She shouldn't be the one to give Carolyn hope. A reason to live. This was a bad idea, a terrible idea. Nevertheless, she tossed out the offering like a discarded gum wrapper. A wrapper she hoped would catch a wind drift and blow far out of reach for someone to pick up. Then perhaps they would put it in its proper place—the garbage can. This was where the idea belonged.

"You'll come stay with me until you can get back on your feet."

The genuine smile and brief brightness to Carolyn's eyes told Sabrina that maybe the lifeline she'd thrown wouldn't blow up in her face. "Thank you," Carolyn replied.

Sabrina needed to set boundaries. "Carolyn," she began.

"I know. This doesn't mean we're getting back together. I get it. I've demolished any chance of that when..."

"I care about you, but yes, that won't be in the cards for us. Getting healthy should be your only focus."

Carolyn nodded. "I think they'll let me out of here in a few days now that I have somewhere to go. That seemed to be the only thing they cared about. I guess they need the bed I'm in. As always, I seem to just take up space," she added with bitterness.

Sabrina didn't know how to respond so she squeezed Carolyn's hand and said, "We'll figure it all out. No, you'll figure it all out and I'll support you in that quest."

"Will you stay for a little while longer?" Carolyn pleaded.

Sabrina nodded. "I have to find time to get a blow-up bed. My apartment is small and I only have one bedroom."

"I can crash on the couch. Compared to the places I've been laying my head, I'm sure your apartment will seem like the Taj Mahal."

"Nah. Blow-up beds have come a long way. They even have some that you plug in to an outlet and the device adds air when the mattress deflates. I borrowed one from a colleague when I first moved here and was waiting for my bed to arrive. The thing was impressive, and cheap as I recall when I looked at them online. I thought it might come in handy if my parents ever visited. I never got around to buying one."

"There's no rush since they aren't likely to let me out of here tonight."

"I'll stay until visiting hours are over. How's that?"

"Thanks. You being here means the world to me."

"I know." Despite her better judgment, she kept holding Carolyn's hand. Now was not the time to pull the only support Carolyn had out from under her wobbly foundation.

†

Joey's stomach growled, reminding her that her nervous energy had not propelled her to one of her favorite food hangouts, but had instead caused her to pace her apartment. She needed something more substantial than the snacks she had lying around. She decided to slip out and get something to bring back, and maybe she would get a few extras for Sabrina in case she returned in the next couple of hours. Thai food was easy to reheat. Yeah, that's what she would do.

If Sabrina didn't text her back by the time Joey returned, she'd send another text. She needed to make sure she was all right. This was the longest amount of time they'd not communicated with one another during their overlapping free time. Joey knew Sabrina wasn't working at the clinic and she never napped during the day, so whoever was taking up her time must be important. Joey was dying to know who this mystery person was. Sabrina hadn't lived in Seattle long. Joey didn't think she had another close friend, and she knew Sabrina wasn't seeing anyone.

Grabbing her light rain jacket, she dashed out the door on her mission to bring back food. When she reached the outside, she didn't bother to pull up her hood. A light mist was falling but not enough to warrant covering her head. This was Seattle. People rarely carried umbrellas or pulled up their hoods. The light rain would not drench her and it felt good.

When she reached the Thai restaurant, she looked at the menu trying to decide which item Sabrina would enjoy most. A smile appeared on her face when she realized she knew what Sabrina would order if she were here. Joey chuckled and set the menu down as she greeted the small woman looking quizzically at this crazy person laughing to herself.

"I'll take an order of mango curry with shrimp, please, and make that as light on the spice as you can without ruining the curry. Add a mango curry with chicken and that one can have a bit of fire, not the hottest, somewhere in the middle. Oh, and can you please pack them up to go?"

"Yes. Twenty minutes. Where's your friend?"

Joey smiled. "She had something else to do tonight, so I'm bringing back food for when she returns."

"You wait here?"

"Yeah, I'll hang out over there." Joey pointed to an empty table in the corner.

Joey remembered when they'd ordered Thai before and Sabrina had been adamant about the lowest amount of spice she could order. She replayed the conversation.

"I don't get how Thai is one of your favorite foods, yet you don't tolerate spice, like at all."

Sabrina shrugged. "I can taste a single speck of pepper. My mom would eat jalapenos whole, but I suppose I have far too many taste receptacles. I love curry, but only when the spice is not overpowering. The best Thai restaurants can accommodate people like me. When I was younger, I was an exchange student in the UK. In the 1970s, most of the food there was so bland, except for the Indian food. It was recommended to me and I guess I developed a taste for curry when I was there."

Joey laughed. "Is Indian and Thai really that similar?"

"I don't know. Thai is better because there are other spices like lemongrass, peanut sauce, or coconut milk that make it a lot more tasty than Indian curry, but there's still that curry spice I grew to love. I know, I know, I'm an anomaly."

"In more ways than one." Joey laughed. "I like your unique qualities and perspectives."

The petite woman startled Joey from her thoughts when she approached her table with a large bag. She stood and accepted the dinners. She missed having dinner with Sabrina and the accompanying conversation that always proved interesting. Sabrina was intelligent, witty, and fun without being pretentious. All lethal qualities that spelled trouble to Joey. She was the kind of woman Joey could see herself settling down with after medical school. Would the long wait drive Sabrina away? Surely she had her pick of women and Joey was waiting for a time when Sabrina told her she'd found someone she was serious about. She knew she shouldn't wish for Sabrina to remain alone, but that's exactly the prayer she sent to the universe every single night. A selfish plea that made her feel all the more guilty because Sabrina deserved someone who would put her needs first, not take a back seat to Joey's life aspirations.

†

The sky was dark when Sabrina left the hospital. She'd stayed beyond visiting hours because none of the nurses had kicked her out. They seemed happy someone was there because it made their work easier. A suicidal patient without support always required more attention.

Sabrina hurried to her car, wondering if Joey was still poring over her notes and preparing for the first day of her clerkship. She hadn't appeared nervous but then Joey rarely showed any lack of confidence. Her own doctoral program had trained Sabrina in subtleties and she could pick out nervousness. Very little escaped Joey's carefully constructed facade. If Sabrina wanted to study that fifth pane in an individual's personality, Joey would be a fascinating subject.

Shaking her head, Sabrina chastised herself. Joey wasn't an experiment. She wasn't a bug to place under a microscope to examine for the tiny clues to her real self. No, Joey was becoming a close friend. As much as she dreamed of something more, Sabrina knew that was out of the question for the next few years. After the clerkships there would be her residency. Where she might land was a big deal. Then there was the reality that she'd already signed on the dotted line to work in Forks for a minimum of three years. Forks, Washington. There was no way that Sabrina saw herself moving to the rainiest place in the US. Sabrina didn't know if she had seasonal affective disorder, but Forks could cause that in the sanest person. Normal people needed sunshine and vitamin D to thrive. Joey had sworn it didn't rain that much in Forks and certainly not more than Seattle. Considering Sabrina had fallen in love with the rainy Pacific Northwest, her aversion to Forks seemed silly. She wasn't so keen on the traffic and Joey had glommed onto that little tidbit. Joey.

Why couldn't she get Joey out of her mind? It wouldn't hurt to check and see if she needed a break from her studies.

Sabrina slammed the car door shut after easing into a parking space and hurried into the building. She glanced at her watch. It was still early. She knew Joey wouldn't be in bed yet at 9:30.

A crooked smile greeted Sabrina after she knocked on Joey's door. "Hey you. Hungry?"

"Starved. I didn't want to take a chance on..." Sabrina stopped talking. She wasn't sure how much of her evening she wanted to share with Joey. She knew she would have to provide some explanation. They were friends and did spend a lot of time together. Joey would have questions about Carolyn once they discharged her and she came to the apartment to stay. How long she would be there was anyone's guess.

"Come on in. I got Thai and I might have ordered extra."

Sabrina touched Joey's arm and squeezed before entering the familiar space. "Thanks."

Joey quirked her eyebrow. "I should probably mind my own business and not ask questions, but I can't help myself. You seem a little...off tonight. Not exactly sad, but..."

"Do you have any alcohol?" Sabrina asked.

"I do. That bad, huh?"

"The past never stays in the past. Whoever said when your past rings you up, don't answer because they sure as shit have nothing new to say, is not living in the real world."

Joey chuckled. "I'm not sure I've quite heard that particular quote in the same manner."

"I took a small poetic license and paraphrased."

"I rather like the one where if we don't learn from our past, we're destined to make the same mistakes. Are you in the midst of making a whopper of a mistake?"

Sabrina plopped onto Joey's couch. "Maybe. Wine, hard cider, I'll even take a beer. Hit me, please."

"I might have bought several pineapple hard ciders. Not sure how well it goes with reheated mango curry, but I know your weakness for the stuff."

Sabrina could feel her mood lighten. "Aw, you got my favorite, didn't you? Mango and pineapple. Why not? Sounds like the perfect combo."

"You sit back and relax. Let Doctor Joey take care of you."

Sabrina leaned her head back on the couch and sighed. She listened as Joey opened the refrigerator, popped the top on the cider, and placed her late dinner into the microwave for reheating. All common sounds she recognized as Joey tending to her needs like she'd done before when they hung out. Sabrina was a natural caretaker with someone's emotional state, but Joey was the real caretaker in many other ways.

"Why are you so good to me? A girl could get spoiled and never want to leave, you know?"

"That's the plan," Joey mumbled.

Sabrina played along like she hadn't heard Joey's response. "What?" She knew that Joey had spoken those words so softly with her back turned because she believed Sabrina hadn't heard them.

"Oh, I said that's my evil plan because after med school I need a wife and will expect payback for the years I took care of you."

Sabrina laughed. "Somehow I think you just embellished on the original response."

"Clarification, not an embellishment." Joey set the hard cider on a coaster and turned toward the sound of the ding from the microwave. "Your feast appears to be ready. Chopsticks?"

"Uh huh," Sabrina answered absently after taking a swig of her drink. "Mmm. This hits the spot. You know how many years I took to master chop sticks? Now I almost prefer them to any other eating utensil."

Joey opened a drawer and retrieved the chopsticks. Grabbing the takeout container from the microwave she speared the sticks into the container.

"I think they are better for modulating one's food intake. A fork or a spoon generates more of the shovel effect."

"What? I don't get a dinner plate?" Sabrina joked.

"We never use dinner plates. You know my stance on that. More dishes mean more wasteful use of water and soap." Setting the container on the coffee table, Joey added, "Besides, takeout Thai was designed to eat right from the container. It's a universal rule."

"I know. Just giving you a little crap because I can. I can't believe my best friend is both a health nut and an environmental crusader."

Joey tilted her head. "Best friend? Is that what I am?"

"I know, that sounds so childish doesn't it? I never thought I would use that vernacular. I wasn't one of those silly high school girls who had a best friend glued to my hip. You know, the ones that couldn't take a piss without the other person tagging along. I was the odd nerdy type that barely tolerated people in my stratosphere. This is like a whole new thing for me. I think I'm trying to relive my youth and you, my dear, are going to help me."

"Fine, but I reserve the right to redefine our relationship down the road. Isn't that what happens in every book, lesbian web series, lesbian movie, etcetera, etcetera, etcetera? We'll finally realize that, all those years, we were madly in love with each other and not the hunky guy."

Joey joined Sabrina on the couch and turned to face her as Sabrina took a small bite of food.

"But we already know we like women and not men," Sabrina argued.

"Minor details."

"And I'm sure all those books, lesbian web series, etcetera, feature women in their teens."

"No, they don't. There are plenty of them that feature women in their twenties or thirties even."

Sabrina roared with laughter. "So that's what you do when we aren't hanging out. You watch all those lesbian web series."

"Maybe. They're kind of addictive and mindless entertainment. They're the perfect length. Most of the time they are less than ten minutes long. I can watch one or two, get my fix, and then I'm totally rejuvenated and ready to hit the books again."

Sabrina grabbed a shrimp with her chopsticks and put the succulent morsel in her mouth. "By the way, this is scrumptious. Thank you."

"My pleasure. Now...quit stalling and tell me what's up?"

Sabrina took a long pull from her cider and met Joey's eyes. "My ex was in trouble."

Joey frowned. "The ex you moved across the country to get away from? Why would you need to go out...no, no, no, she didn't?"

"Um, surprise. She's here in Seattle."

"Fuck me. Really?"

"She tried to commit suicide. She's at the UW Medical Center. I offered her a place to stay until she gets back on her feet." The words rushed out of Sabrina's mouth. They were strung together like a tangled set of Christmas lights.

"Wow. Okay. I take it she doesn't have family or other friends she could call."

Sabrina shook her head. "I think her mother would want to know, but Carolyn is adamant about not calling her. I think she's afraid of her father's reaction. He's a real son of a bitch."

"Does he have to know? Why can't you call her mother without her father getting involved?"

"He controls everything, and would find out. He monitors her cell phone, controls the money..."

"Oh. So how bad? A serious attempt? Or was it more of a cry for help?"

"I think it was dumb luck she survived. She also has drug issues. I'm not sure how to deal with those. Maybe she should go straight to rehab from the hospital and not my place. I don't know the first thing about detox or whatever it's called when you flush drugs from your system. I know about mental health issues, but I can't be her therapist either. I know, I know. This is a horrid idea, but you should have seen her." Sabrina lowered her head, clasped her hands together, and tapped them against her chin. "I've never seen her so fragile. So alone. I loved her once. I can't abandon her."

Joey scooted closer to Sabrina and gathered her in her arms. Sabrina laid her head against Joey's shoulder.

"No, of course not. I'll help. With the medical part if there is something we should do for detox. Can I ask how she, um..."

Sabrina lifted her head. "Slit wrists. The long way. The bandage almost covers her arm."

"Okay, I'll make sure we take care of the wounds."

"Thanks, Joey." Sabrina returned to her previous position with her head resting on Joey's shoulder.

"What are besties for, anyway? You know I'll help." Joey tightened her hold for a split second and gave Sabrina a comforting squeeze.

Sabrina was trying to ignore how Joey's embrace and reassuring touch impacted her. She didn't need the additional complication right now. Sabrina lifted her head again and moved away to create a little distance, although Joey's arm stubbornly remained around her shoulder, as if the connection was just as important to Joey.

"Hey, how about I do your laundry for the next month as payment for helping out."

Joey grinned. "You want the perfect excuse to get your paws on my boi shorts. You obviously believe that with so many, I won't notice one or two missing. Well, you're right, I probably wouldn't."

Shit, now I have her undies burned into my brain. And, of course, the notion of nicking one of them. Sabrina grinned like a fool.

"Busted, but I will take you up on that generous offer, because I loathe doing laundry." Joey jumped up. "I was hoping that my incredible charms would get to you and that you'd make this offer. I've been saving up for this day. Two full duffel bags and an armful of strays coming up." She walked out of the living room and into her bedroom, returning a few minutes later with overflowing bags of clothing looped over each arm and several garments held against her stomach. She dumped them to the side of the couch next to Sabrina. "I can help carry them to the laundry room tomorrow morning. Just come knocking on my door when you're ready."

"It'll have to be early. I have to work tomorrow and then I need to go to the hospital..."

"Early is perfect."

"Speaking of which, I better go home now. It looks like I will need to get up at the ass crack of dawn to—"

"Oh, shit. I'm sorry. What's a few more days? I still have a few pairs of boi shorts that are clean. You don't have to do them tomorrow. Do you work every day this week?"

Sabrina shook her head. "No. Okay, Wednesday it is. You can keep your stinky pile of clothes until then. I still should be going." Sabrina stood. "Hey, I'm sorry. I forgot to wish you good luck tomorrow. Emergency medicine should be great fun. I know you're looking forward to this clerkship." Sabrina opened her arms and Joey eagerly accepted her offering of a hug before Sabrina left.

After Joey stepped away from Sabrina's embrace, she replied, "I am anticipating this clerkship. Sometimes I'm an adrenaline junkie and this will satisfy my urge. Besides, I haven't decided whether I'll stick with family medicine. The good news is that Forks would let me pick up shifts in their ED if that's what I'm interested in."

"You'll be fabo in both." Sabrina left Joey's apartment a little lighter than when she'd first arrived.

Chapter Seven

Joey's first day in the ED was uneventful. In fact, it was rather slow. She supposed there would be exciting days and others that were beyond boring. Today was one of those very unremarkable days. She wondered if she was a bad person for hoping that she might experience one of those crazy days so she could legitimately decide if emergency medicine might be in her future. As she hung around the nurses' station joking with the staff she was going to spend most of her time with, she took this opportunity to ask about Suboxone treatment. If Joey was going to try to help Sabrina's ex, she needed to know if a prescription for Suboxone would be a good choice. Joey had her doubts. From what she'd learned after doing a fair amount of online research, and talking with one of the doctors who had strong feelings about the drug, Joey didn't think it was such a good idea to use this treatment as a method for lessening the symptoms.

After her shift, Joey made a beeline to Sabrina's apartment, armed with information on how to help Carolyn that did not include a regimen of Suboxone as a replacement drug. Her main concern was the side effects and the fact the doctors did not recommend the drug for anyone struggling with depression. Maybe Sabrina already knew this. She worked in the mental health field and had interacted with individuals struggling with drug abuse issues.

When no answer came after three quick knocks on Sabrina's door, Joey smacked her head. Of course—Sabrina had gone to the hospital after work. Joey wondered whether she should wait or send a quick text to see if she should zip over to the hospital and lend her support. One night free from her incessant research and reading from various medical journals after her first day of a clerkship would not kill her.

Pulling her phone from her back pocket, she thumbed a quick text and then sat down to wait for a response.

Taking the night off, want some company at the hospital?

Joey waited impatiently for a response as she looked for the shimmering triple dots. She decided a text was stupid. She should make a phone call. What was the obsession with text over phone calls, anyway? Hearing another person's voice was more personal. Why was she always putting that barrier between herself and the people she cared for? Why did anyone? She was a product of the new generation, she supposed. *Fuck that, I'm calling her.*

Thank God Sabrina answered after two rings. "Hey you. Sorry I didn't text back, I was walking and thought I should wait until I got to her room."

Joey smiled. It was obvious Sabrina was not ignoring her. She needed to be more undemanding. "People don't use the phone enough in the way it was originally intended. A text is so impersonal. I've stopped being the poster child for our generation. Have you ever wondered why texting is so popular nowadays? Are we that afraid of human connections?"

The tinkling of Sabrina's laughter came through from the other end of the phone and she replied, "Dramatic much? Maybe I should change my dissertation topic to texting as a means of avoiding emotional engagement."

"Do you hate your topic that much? I'm kinda hurt you haven't let me read what you have so far. It seems interesting enough."

"Interesting conversation to have over the phone, don't you think? Especially since we're talking about avoiding deep and meaningful interactions through the use of technology. I don't think the purpose for your call is to discuss my faltering dissertation. Right now it's on the brink of death, and an influx of life-saving medicine is needed to bring it back. Or I could admit defeat, do the kind thing and embrace the concept of death with dignity. That's the real reason I haven't shared it with you."

Joey chuckled. "Fair enough. Look, the reason I called is I want to follow up on my text. How about I come to the hospital tonight?"

Joey could hear the hesitation on the other end of the phone. Three seconds is a long time. Longer than people realize.

"I don't know, Joey. I can't decide if that would be a good or bad idea. She's fragile now and your presence might signal how far along I've traveled. She knows I moved on..."

"It's not like we have that kind of relationship."

"No, but—"

"I get it. Bad idea. So, does this mean you don't want help with the medical stuff? I asked around about withdrawal and the use of Suboxone. There are varied opinions, and I'd be happy to tell you about what I learned. I want to help."

Sabrina sighed. "I know and I appreciate that. How about if we talk about this later? Can I come see you tonight after visitation is over? I suspect we'll decide on a solid plan by then. The forty-eight-hour hold will be over soon..."

"Sure, but I just want to say, I believe if they offer Suboxone, that would be a bad recommendation for a lot of reasons."

"Noted. I know you do thorough research and I was of the same mind, anyway. There aren't great options for Carolyn. She can be stubborn. Look, I'll come by later. I'm almost to her room. I gotta go."

"Okay. I'll be waiting. I'm here for you."

"Thanks."

Joey placed the phone on her coffee table and looked up at her ceiling. The answers didn't magically appear for her. She wondered if she should get dinner for Sabrina. This was fast becoming a habit. She jumped up and decided that yes, she should, because that was one thing she knew for sure would help.

†

Carolyn didn't look markedly better when Sabrina pushed open the door and entered the room. Her pale face and sunken sockets telegraphed how far she'd fallen. Sabrina hesitantly approached the bedside and sat in the chair as Carolyn turned to face her.

"I've lost the one thing I had going for me, haven't I?" she asked.

"The one thing?" Sabrina parroted.

"Yeah, my looks. Although my father might be pleased with that. He blamed my slutty ways on my beauty." Carolyn coughed and continued, "He once said it would have been better if I'd been born ugly. But no, I had to grow up to be the spitting image of her. He never believed Mother wasn't cheating on him. Paranoid bastard."

Sabrina couldn't stop herself. She pushed back a sweaty lock of Carolyn's once-lustrous blond hair. "You haven't lost your beauty. Contrary to popular belief, although you tried to hide it, you possess a lot of inner beauty. Sure, I was initially attracted to your outward appearance, I won't deny that. But, Carolyn, and this is a big but, I fell in love with the person you are in here." Sabrina placed her hand on Carolyn's heart.

"I fucked everything up, didn't I? An insatiable need for love to fill a hole that nobody came close to filling is a hard thing to fight."

"Therapy helps. It can help you. I hope this time you won't fight it. I used to study you and watch you when you didn't know it. I would observe that part of yourself you didn't want people to see. You know what I remember?"

"Tell me. I need something nice to hang onto."

"I will. I'd listen when you talked to those feral kittens you used to feed. I could never get them to come to me, but you could. You were like the cat whisperer. I decided right then and there, you were a good person no matter how many times you acted out. People who are kind to animals have this generosity inside they can't hide from the world."

"How can anyone resist an innocent little life? Most people are kind to kittens, that's not some wonderful trait."

"Not true. At least not in the way that you were with them. You were also magic with kids—especially troubled kids. I always wanted you to go back to school and do something with your gift. It's not too late, you know."

"Ha, if I got a degree in social work or whatever, who would hire a former drug addict with a side of sex addiction."

"People turn their lives around all the time."

"Is it too late for us?" Carolyn asked.

Sabrina looked away. "They say the best thing to do is change people, places, and things. I heard that somewhere. I'm one of those people you should change and have a go at a new start."

"You met someone, didn't you?"

"It's complicated. I won't lie to you and tell you no, but I don't think it will go anywhere." Sabrina returned her eyes to Carolyn's.

"Don't be so sure about that, Sabrina. You're a hard woman to resist and easy to fall in love with. I did love you. Hon, you have to know that." She reached for Sabrina's hand and Sabrina allowed herself this small connection.

"I do and I did, but that was not enough. I can't be that savior for you. That would not be fair to either one of us. Change is not always bad, you know. Evolution and all." She smiled.

Carolyn smiled back and Sabrina glimpsed the old Carolyn. The beautiful woman she'd fallen so hard and fast for.

"So...when do I meet this woman? You deserve to be happy and I promise I won't fuck that up for you. I think I owe you. The least I can do is not get in the middle of whatever may transpire between you two."

Sabrina squeezed Carolyn's hand. "I see the healing is beginning. You're becoming the change you want to be."

"Hitting rock bottom will do that for you. I've been mulling my choices and my life. I don't want to continue to repeat past crimes and mistakes. Hell, I might want to do this for no other reason than to stick it to my father. Become something he's always told me I could never be—a decent human being capable of putting someone else first. Oh, and I'll definitely have to work on that monogamy thing. That would chafe his hide. He hates when he's wrong."

Sabrina furrowed her brow. "Don't make changes to spite your father."

"Kidding, well sort of. I know I need to make changes for myself, but can't I appreciate the side benefits"—Carolyn held up her hand to indicate a tiny amount—"just a smidgen?"

"Fine. Your father is a smug bastard. Your mother, on the other hand, deserves to find out what happened. I get that you don't want her to know because then your father would hear about it...but...you have to believe that she's worrying about you. How about we come up with a compromise position?"

"I'm listening."

"After you get back on your feet, you call her and tell her where you are and how you're doing."

"You have that much faith in my ability to turn my life around?"

"I do. I always have. I simply stopped thinking it was a good idea to be there with you when you did."

†

Joey invited Sabrina into her apartment and was relieved it was still early in the evening. She presumed things had gone well at the hospital and was eager to receive an update.

"I brought sushi." Sabrina held up a white bag.

Joey burst out laughing. "Great minds." She walked into the small kitchen and flipped open the Styrofoam containers. Turning them around, she showed what was inside to Sabrina. "Well, we'll either stuff ourselves to the gill or have a lot of leftovers. Believe it or not, I have eaten sushi for breakfast before."

Sabrina chuckled. "Oh, I believe that. Although, I suspect you toss away the white rice as something fundamentally destructive to your perfect body."

Joey raised her eyebrow. "Perfect body, huh? Okay, new topic. Want some sake?"

"Yup, I do. Sushi must accompany sake. That's the rule."

"Will you tell me what happened tonight with Carolyn? Do you have a plan for her recovery?" Joey reached into her refrigerator and pulled out a bottle of sake.

Sabrina looked sad. "We do. I'd rather she made a different decision, but I have to respect her wishes."

"Let me guess. She doesn't want to ride out the withdrawal amongst the sterile walls of a hospital room. You know, I'll help, but do you think that's the best idea? She might depend on your kind heart a little too much. It could be a way to get you back. It's a real high when someone needs you."

"Hey, who's the shrink here? I don't think so. We talked about it."

"Oh, do tell." Joey sauntered over and placed the alcohol on the table.

"She was sincere when she said she wants to meet you."

"Now that is so intriguing. Should I read between the lines? Are you trying to tell me that…"

"No, no, I'm not suggesting, um…sorry. You're important to me, that's all."

"Okay, I'll take important. You want chopsticks or shall we eat sushi the way it was intended? I often think of sushi as finger food. I don't need no stinkin' chopsticks," she said in a bad imitation of an outlaw accent.

"Funny. Seems uncouth to me. I'll take chopsticks, please."

Joey slammed her hand against her chest. "I am so wounded. I believe you just called me uncouth."

"Thanks for the breather and letting me off the hook. I know you went down this little side road for a reason."

"Ooh, busted. Maybe I will develop a decent bedside manner after all." Joey grabbed two sets of chopsticks from the drawer and gathered the sushi, setting both on the table. "Oops, I forgot the tiny little cups for the sake. That would be a double whammy, to drink out of the bottle, huh?"

"Absolutely. You know that is only allowed when we pass around the bottle of whiskey. Whiskey is the only drink that begs to be consumed straight from the bottle. Janis Joplin taught me that."

"Seriously? Was that really Janis's drink of choice?"

"I think so, but I can only go by what my mother passed along regarding stories from the glory days of feminism." Sabrina rolled her eyes.

"Was your mom a hippy or one of those granola types?"

"Both, I think."

"Now I really want to meet her."

"She'd like you. You have that little rebel, bad ass side to you. I think she can relate to that from her youth."

"Hmm, okay. So, I take it she has no problem with your sexuality."

"Are you kidding? She threw me a coming out party. Said she was so relieved I wouldn't fall into the trap of male oppression."

"Is she a lesbian?"

"God, no. She would confess, when she was tipsy, that she always had a weakness for dick and wondered why the goddess had to be so cruel."

Joey plopped on the couch and erupted into a fit of laughter. She picked up the chopsticks and selected a piece of fish from the sashimi laid out in one container. "I want to meet her now."

"So, if it's not too painful to talk about. What was your mother like?" Sabrina asked.

Joey sat back against the cushion of her couch and laid her head on the top.

"She was an intellectual. When the doctor gave her the diagnosis, she treated the cancer like a minor interruption in her life plans. It wasn't until the end when I saw a tiny crack in her veneer. It's not like I don't believe she loved me, but she wasn't the touchy-feely type. Her quick wit was legendary, and she could be very, very, funny. I guess I'm an amalgamation between my mother and father. My father was the exact opposite. He was very affectionate. They balanced one another. And yet, that depth of emotion was too great for him. He couldn't handle seeing my mother in her last stages."

"Wow. Okay, let me think." Sabrina lifted her head from the back of the couch. "Tell me a favorite story about your mother. Something you'll never forget."

"Oh, that would have to be the Sex Ed lecture."

Sabrina laughed. "This will be good."

"See, I grew up in a conservative town. We lived in an upper-middle-class neighborhood and my mother was rather clinical and blasé about things such as sex. She always treated me like an adult, even when I was younger. Unfortunately, this bled over to my friends. One day we were giggling over a *Playboy* magazine. At the time most of my friends were boys. Anyway, my mother caught us and gave a full-on lecture of the birds and bees. It was dispassionate and clinical, but that did not stop the other mothers from having a full-on tizzy fit over it."

Sabrina laughed. "How did you know the other mothers were unhappy?"

"Well, after the fifth phone call, my father asked. 'Now why did you have to take it upon yourself to educate those kids?'"

"My mother couldn't understand why it was such a big deal. She thought if kids were curious about sex, why not answer their questions rather than make it a big secret, or worse a taboo. My father disagreed. Vehemently, I might add."

"Hmm. It's funny how men get uncomfortable having *the talk*, even with their sons," Sabrina noted.

"Yeah, that was true in our house. Mom was cool like that. She took everything in stride. Nothing seemed to ruffle her. Kinda like you. I wanted her to react to me being a lesbian. She didn't. It almost felt like I'd told her I was planning to take the bus instead of my bike to school. I think she might have said something like, 'okay,' and then returned to whatever she was doing. It's not like she wasn't interested in hearing about my day; she didn't think me being a lesbian was a big deal. She cared more about how I was doing in school. I don't mean to suggest she was an uninvolved parent because that couldn't be further from the truth. She had a way with picking what was important and what was not."

"Was that okay with you?"

"Yeah, it was. I think I admired my mother more than my father. Unfortunately, that might make me more emotionally stunted than is good for me. I'm prone to taking a more detached, clinical approach to anything remotely complicated. And that includes emotions. I'm working on that. You know, a living, breathing, work in progress." Joey grinned and then shifted gears. "Hey, are you off tomorrow?"

"Yeah, I took off the rest of the week. I told them I had a personal issue to resolve. They don't ask questions. I appreciate that about work. I suppose when you get all up in everyone's business for a living, you don't have enough energy to do that to your coworkers. Besides, I think we are all good at recognizing when someone erects those barriers. My message was clear. Don't ask and I ain't gonna tell."

"I'll come over right after my shift. We'll definitely have to put our trip to Forks on the back burner again." Joey tried to keep the disappointment from her voice.

"I'm sorry, yeah. I do want to go with you after things settle a bit. Thanks for understanding."

"Of course. I sure hope you know what you're getting yourself into. Withdrawal is a real bitch, depending on how long she's been addicted and to what drugs."

"From the looks of her, yeah, it will be rough. I believe they are managing her withdrawal right now with some kind of drug. I didn't ask which one. I suspect that after the hospital discharges her, the symptoms will hit her with a force I might not be prepared for. She's not a great candidate for Suboxone, so I don't think that's what they've been giving her. You were right about that, but she is a good prospect for medically monitored care. Unfortunately, she is staunchly refusing that. She's no dummy. She knows this will be tough. I think it's her form of self-punishment for prior wrongs. I don't recommend that course of action, but I would never decide for someone else."

"Even if those decisions will profoundly impact you?"

"Yup. Maybe I am punishing myself for not recognizing her cries for help. I was too close and erroneously thought it was her need for something new and shiny. Turns out I was wrong."

"Perfection is a complete turnoff. I'm glad you're human. I was beginning to worry." Joey smiled.

CHAPTER EIGHT

Sabrina would be lying to herself if she didn't admit that agreeing to Carolyn's wishes would be a terrible idea. The doctors said as much, but they couldn't keep her or force her to choose another avenue. Carolyn was still very fragile both emotionally and physically. Sabrina wasn't sure which worried her more. It was time to adopt her own cheery facade. Before entering the room, Sabrina plastered a smile on her face.

The nurse had a disapproving look as she completed the discharge papers. She reminded Sabrina of a scorpion ready to strike with her pursed lips and squinted eyes. She'd mumbled something about noting that Carolyn was leaving AMA. Against medical advice. That was hospital-speak for doing something that was not at all recommended.

Carolyn was down to less than 100 pounds, dripping wet. Getting her to put on some weight while fighting withdrawal was not going to be easy. Sabrina wondered if she could convince Carolyn to accept home care. At least the home care nurse could hook her up to an IV. Visions of Carolyn dying from dehydration or starvation haunted Sabrina. She'd promised, but now that they were rolling Carolyn out the door, she wasn't sure she could live up to that promise.

After Carolyn buckled herself in, pushing away Sabrina's hand, insisting she wasn't a child, Sabrina slid into the driver's side and took in a big breath.

"Look, I know I agreed to this, but—"

"You promised and you never break a promise."

"Can I at least call in reinforcements? Please?" Sabrina ventured a glance at Carolyn and felt her eyes water.

"I don't want a strange home health nurse poking at me."

"Oh, but you'll stick a needle in yourself." Sabrina's hand flew to her mouth. "God, I'm sorry. Really, I am. That was..."

"True and honest. Thanks. I need that. I'd rather have your anger than your pity."

Sabrina took Carolyn's hand and confessed, "I'm scared. I don't have medical training. What if something goes horribly wrong and you end up...I can't even say it."

"Dying. We're all going to die someday. Some of us sooner than others, but I promise, I'll feel like I want to die but I won't. I've seen people go through withdrawal and it isn't a walk in the park, but most of the time they live. I'm dying"—Carolyn grinned—"not literally, to meet this Joey person. She has enough medical training to keep you from your guilt if something goes sideways."

"How can you be so cavalier about your life?"

104

"That's just it, Sabrina. It's my life, not yours and you promised to let me decide about this."

"Stupidest thing I've ever done."

"Nope. I have a good feeling about all of this. I think it is the best thing you've ever done. I want to face the consequences of my choices head on and I don't want you to save me. All I ask is for you to stand beside me and support my decisions. I'd kind of like you there when I reach the other side. Not death. I mean the other side of this rock bottom place I've been. Oh, and maybe you can hold my hair back when I'm puking my guts out."

Sabrina returned her face forward and eased out of the parking lot. "I can do that. I still remember when I had that awful norovirus and no matter how bad your gag reflex was, you were there for me. That's another one of those times where your inner beauty was shining through. By the way, have you ever thought about becoming a nurse? You have that caring side that needs a place to dance."

"Psht...gag reflex, remember? Can't handle other people's bodily fluids." Carolyn's head settled on the headrest.

"Oh right, yeah, there was that." Sabrina glanced at Carolyn before looking over her shoulder and changing lanes. She noted the haggard look as Carolyn seemed too tired to hold her head up.

When Carolyn chuckled, the sound of her laughter encouraged Sabrina. It seemed genuine. Maybe things would work out. She wanted to call Joey. She needed a little more reassurance.

"You can call her, you know. I won't fall apart knowing there is someone else you care about. Love from what I've gathered. Again, I'm not as oblivious as you think I am."

"I never said you were. We're just friends."

"Sure you are. What's that pane in that window thingy again? You know, the one where everyone else can see it, but you can't. Hello, clueless pane. Guess what? You've captured another guileless soul."

"Wow, I never thought you were ever listening to my babble."

"I listened. More than you think."

"I am learning more about you now than I did in the entire five years we were together," Sabrina noted with interest.

"Maybe you were the one without listening skills."

Sabrina frowned. "That was harsh."

"I never meant you weren't good at your job or vocation. You have impeccable listening skills with those you aren't involved with."

"Touché. I suppose that is something I will need to work a little harder on."

"I think you have already. I've seen a few changes. You're more focused. Self-reflection is a good thing, Sabrina. Painful sometimes, but good."

"Okay, I'm going to revise my earlier declaration. You should definitely pursue a job in counseling or mental health. That is your true calling. With youth, I think." Sabrina nodded her head. "Yes, with kids."

"That's the second time you've said that. We'll see. First, I've got to survive the next seven days." Carolyn touched Sabrina's arm after Sabrina tensed. "Kidding."

"Not funny. Stop with the dark humor, please. It's unsettling."

"All right. That's fair. I've already hurt you enough. I don't want to continue to do that. I'm sorry. Old coping mechanism."

"I know. I did pay a little attention. I know that about you." Sabrina grinned.

"Touché back at you."

†

The sweating had already started. Joey's practiced eye registered that right after seeing the look of panic on Sabrina's face. She'd barely knocked when the door opened to Sabrina's wild-eyed, messy hair, appearance. She suspected that Sabrina had nervously run her hand through her hair multiple times throughout the day.

Holding up the plastic grocery bag, Joey announced, "I come bearing gifts." She walked into the room and kneeled down in front of the sickly-looking woman she assumed was Carolyn. "Hey, I'm Joey. Do you mind if I do a quick assessment? Then I will entice you to eat even if you're nauseous right now."

"Carolyn." She offered a shaking hand.

Joey took her wrist looking for a place to press her thumb against the pulse point. "Good to meet you." She was all business now. "How long have you had the sweats?"

"For the last two hours," Sabrina answered.

"Nauseous?"

"Check." Carolyn grimaced.

"Okay. Stage one is in full swing. Are you sure you want to do this without medical assistance? It will get a lot worse before it gets better. You know this can be dangerous, right?"

Carolyn nodded; her jaw set hard in what Joey recognized as conviction. A small amount of admiration snuck in as she eyed Sabrina's ex. There had to be several redeeming qualities if a woman as wonderful as Sabrina had spent five years with her.

"I hate seeing Sabrina look like this. I sure hope you're here to support her."

"I'm here for both of you. Okay?" Joey pulled a Boost from the grocery bag she'd set down before greeting Carolyn.

"Don't let the label fool you. This stuff is something you need right now. Some soothing tea will make a great side dish." Joey tossed a box of organic tea to Sabrina who was biting her lip. "Later, we'll dive into this yummy high-fiber salad full of nutrition. but we can't afford to have you lose more body mass, thus the Boost."

"I know I feel like I'm ninety years old, but do I look like a senior citizen? Boost? Who the hell comes up with names like that? It tastes and looks like chalk. They should call it chalkolate shake." Carolyn emphasized the chalk in her new title.

"I'll send the company a memo with your suggestion. I'm sure they'll rush right out and change the name on millions of products on the shelf right now." Joey grinned.

"Sarcasm. I like her already."

"Well, it was my minor in college. Or rather, I claim it as my second language. Can I look underneath those bandages of yours?"

"You want to look at my naked wrists? I insist you buy me dinner first."

Joey grinned. "I did, remember the Boost and yummy salad for later if you're up to it."

"Oh, right, yes. This one's a keeper, Sabrina."

"How's that tea coming? I think I want one of those rolling stools. Squatting like this is killing my knees. Maybe I should chug the Boost, I'm definitely feeling my advancing age. All that softball in high school."

"You're a walking cliché, you know," Carolyn added, then scrunched her face in pain.

Sabrina brought a steaming cup of tea and set it down in front of Carolyn. "I added a fair amount of honey."

"Good, more calories are helpful. Okay, no more entertaining the guest. I'll check to make sure your wrists aren't infected or heading in that direction, and then the procrastination ends with you slurping down the dinner I bought you. I like to do things backwards. Get your wrists naked first and then offer dinner. If you sit up now, you can lie down later. I promise." Joey helped Carolyn sit.

Carolyn's hands shook as she wiped the sweat away.

Sabrina carefully sat on the couch next to Carolyn and lifted the cup to her lips. "It might still be a little hot." She put the cup down. "Maybe we should wait 'til it cools."

Joey nodded and took one of Carolyn's wrists in her hands as she carefully unwrapped the bandages. She wondered if Sabrina caught her intake of air as she looked at the long horizontal line of stitches. Carolyn was not messing around. She had wanted to die. There was no doubt in Joey's mind that luck was the only thing keeping her in this world right now.

"Did they give you supplies?" Joey asked. She was happy to see there were no signs of infection.

"Yeah. Gauze, cream, the works," Sabrina answered.

"Could you get them for me? I'll redress this after I've had a chance to look at its twin on her other arm."

"So, Doc, will I live?"

"Yup, you will." Joey looked directly in her eyes.

†

After they'd settled Carolyn in Sabrina's bed, Sabrina glanced at Joey. She looked as if there was a painful question at the tip of her tongue. Sabrina tugged on Joey's arm and pulled her into the living room.

"Okay, spit it out," she whispered. "There's a question in the beautifully complicated brain of yours that for some reason you're afraid to ask."

"Not afraid exactly, but I don't know how you'll take it and it might be none of my business," Joey said.

Sabrina pointed to the couch. "Sit. You've never been too shy to ask me anything or offer your sometimes unsolicited perspectives."

"Unsolicited? What are you talking about? We talk about everything. Freely. I thought you liked hearing my opinions and thoughts, even when they differ from yours."

"Relax. I do. I was referring to our first meeting. Does, 'I know every fine ass in this building, I would have recognized yours' ring a bell with you?" Sabrina thought it was adorable that Joey now winced in response to her trip down memory lane. She smiled to soften the blow.

"Not one of my finer moments, I admit. Okay, I'm going to spit it out as you so eloquently put earlier. You only have one bedroom. Where are you going to sleep?"

"In my bed, of course."

"Oh. I didn't realize you two were trying to make a go of it again." Joey stared ahead and made the perfect impression of a little girl who'd lost the ice cream from her cone.

110

"We aren't, you ninny. I have to make sure she's okay and I can't really do that from the living room. I don't know that she has the energy to come get me if something goes terribly wrong. I can sleep in the same bed with someone without having sex, you know. Why, is that a talent you haven't mastered yet?"

"I have other more interesting talents you've yet to experience." Joey wiggled her eyebrows for effect. "You want me to stay out here on the couch in case you need a second medical opinion?" Joey asked.

"Nah. Thanks for coming over and bringing the sustenance. I should give you a ton of money considering I haven't been able to pay you back via laundry duty. I promise that after the bulk of this...um...I don't know what to call it." Sabrina shook her head in defeat. "Maybe by the weekend I can sneak down to the laundry room."

"Don't worry about it. I still have an entire week or more of clean underwear. I'm saving the extra bag of dirty ones just for you. I'll add them to the two overflowing duffels." Joey took several steps forward and pulled Sabrina into her arms to hug her. After they broke apart, she stayed only inches away and Sabrina thought for sure she was going to kiss her. Instead, she placed her forehead against Sabrina's. Sighing loudly, she lifted her head and abruptly turned away, taking several steps back before mumbling, "Sorry."

Sabrina brushed her hand against Joey's cheek and then kissed it. "Nothing to be sorry for. Sleep well, Joey."

"You too. See ya tomorrow night. Same bat time, same bat channel." Then Joey was gone. Sabrina wondered if she had Ninja blood in her after she'd left the apartment quietly and quickly.

Sabrina walked into her bedroom and found a shivering Carolyn moaning softly. She crawled into bed and put her arms around her ex who was in a kind of hell Sabrina knew she'd never understand or experience for herself. The closest she'd ever come to that was when she'd had that nasty norovirus and Carolyn had been there for her. She knew it wasn't the same. She didn't owe Carolyn for taking care of her back then. Sabrina knew she wanted to be there for Carolyn. She still loved her and that was a revelation she didn't want to analyze too deeply. Not now. Not when she had all those confusing and complicated feelings for Joey. *What did Scarlett O'Hara say? Oh yeah, "tomorrow is another day." Or some such shit like that.*

"Oh, God, I'm sorry, but I think I'm going to be sick again," Carolyn whispered before rolling over and puking in the garbage can.

Sabrina held her hair back and after she'd finished went into the bathroom to collect a towel and a washcloth. She prayed this part of Carolyn's recovery would not last too long and that after all this pain, she wouldn't return to the drugs. She'd read the dangers of detoxing at home and the biggest one of all was a relapse with deadly consequences.

CHAPTER NINE

When Joey arrived back at her apartment after her second shift in the ED, she almost turned back around when she saw Maribel smoking a cigarette in the front stoop. Joey hated the taste of cigarettes. Kissing an ashtray was what she'd always said when Maribel came over and had recently smoked. It was almost a libido killer, but Joey had to admit Maribel had a talented tongue. Something she hadn't partaken in for quite some time. Oh, who was she kidding? She hadn't slept with Maribel since the day in the laundry room when she'd met Sabrina.

"Hey." Maribel sucked in a long drag. "Who is the drug addict that Sabrina shuffled into her apartment the other day?"

"None of your fucking business. What, are you stalking her now?"

"Ooh. Touchy, touchy. Must be an ex. I don't think you have anything to worry about. She was a mess. Really unattractive. Although I could see potential. Good bone structure underneath all that pastiness and loss of cushion around those fine bones. I'll bet her hair was once thick and full, too. That is until the beast took hold. I may partake in a few recreational varieties, but never the hard stuff. It wreaks havoc on the looks, you know."

"Don't, Maribel. That was even low for you."

"Okay, okay. Sorry. You seem to bring out my inner bitch sometimes. Why is that?"

Joey shrugged. "It's kinda close to the surface, so it's not very hard." She smiled to take away the sting.

"How about I try that question again, but this time I'll rephrase and maybe I can offer a little assistance. I know that may seem unbelievable, but I don't like to owe people and I think I owe both you and Sabrina. She could have turned me in after that unfortunate incident, but she didn't. As much as I want to hate the little trollop for taking away my good times with you, I can't. The new roommate is doing a round of detox. Am I right?"

Joey nodded.

"She worth saving?"

"Yeah, I think she is. At least that's my preliminary assessment in the brief time I spent in Sabrina's apartment last night."

"In my limited experience, sometimes the caregiver needs a break. It's almost as hard on them as on the one who wants to do their own home detox. Especially if the person cares about the druggie," Maribel noted.

"She does."

"I could offer my sparkling company and maybe a few tricks I've seen work before. I have a friend who is a licensed acupuncturist. I know you're pursuing that Western medicine model. I'll wager you haven't considered the alternative Eastern medicine. I can tell you from personal experience, acupuncture helps with the symptoms. Bet they didn't suggest that option at the hospital, did they?"

Joey grabbed Maribel and kissed her. "You're a genius. Contrary to what you think about me, I do believe in the efficacy of Eastern medicine. I don't think a person has to choose one avenue or another. They can work well together. Thanks, Maribel. I'll talk to Sabrina and see what she thinks."

Maribel took a final drag of her cigarette, tossed it on the sidewalk, and ground it out with her shoe. "You know where to find me when you need a babysitter and my friend to work her miracles."

"Hey, you litter bug, don't leave your butt out here. I was starting to form a positive impression of you, don't ruin that now."

"Fine." Maribel scrunched up her face and bent to pick up the discarded butt, pinching it between her thumb and index finger. Her disgust was apparent, but she opened the door to the building and Joey hoped she would put the trash in an appropriate place.

†

Joey bounded into the building and headed straight for Sabrina's apartment. She thought about asking Sabrina for a key so she could let herself in at night. She rationalized she would give it back after Carolyn was on her feet again.

Shuffling her feet, she waited until Sabrina opened the door. Without a word, Sabrina stepped aside and waved Joey inside. Joey could see the strain on her face. Maybe Maribel was right. Sabrina looked like she could use a short breather.

"Hey you. I was just talking with Maribel and she made a suggestion," Joey said.

Sabrina raised her eyebrow. "Maribel? What? Did she suggest she could score drugs to lessen the symptoms? Thanks, but no thanks. And why the hell would she know about the situation?" Her voice was hard and elevated.

Joey frowned. It was not like Sabrina to snap and be irritable. "You need a break, because that was not you just now. You're usually more Zen when you take me to task. I think she figured it out. I don't know if her motives were pure, but her offer of assistance was genuine. A good idea is a good idea—no matter whose mouth it comes from."

"Sorry," Sabrina grumbled. "I haven't showered yet today. I was too afraid to leave her alone."

Joey sniffed the air. "I noticed." Joey grinned. "Kidding, but go. Take your shower. Sometimes a nice hot shower isn't only for smelling nice. It can be a rejuvenation. I'll look after her. I promise my intentions are pure. I won't off the competition. After you get all sparkly clean, I'll tell you what Maribel said."

Sabrina's hand grazed Joey's cheek. "Thanks. And I'm sorry for my reaction earlier."

"Don't worry about it."

Joey unpacked the groceries she'd brought again. Sabrina had shoved a fistful of money into her hand and Joey reluctantly agreed to take it. It wasn't like either of them were rolling in dough, but she was doing okay. She also had that sweet deal with the hospital in the middle of nowhere that would take care of her mounting student loans. Three years. I can do three years. That was the chant she kept repeating after she felt like she'd made a deal with the devil and her payment was three years in purgatory.

After putting together a nutritious meal and grabbing another Boost and a sports drink, Joey poked her head into the bedroom to see to Carolyn. She was wearing an over-sized hooded sweatshirt that Joey recognized as Sabrina's. Since her hair was still wet, Joey assumed she'd recently come from the shower. Carolyn had propped herself against the headboard. She still looked like death warmed over and Joey wondered if she could get her to eat or drink anything. She hadn't taken in enough nutrition or liquids and Joey was more concerned than she let on. Dehydration was a major risk at this stage.

"I brought dinner again. I doubt you'll be able to resist my gourmet offering tonight."

"Not hungry. I'll probably just puke it up anyway."

"Probably, but maybe a little will absorb into your system before you do. Look, I'll be honest. At this point you're on the verge of a return trip to the hospital. I have an idea to help lessen the symptoms, but I'm not sure I can arrange for it tonight. How do you feel about needles? Little tiny ones to be exact."

Carolyn rolled her eyes. "Seriously?" She pushed her sleeves up over the bandage and displayed the needle marks in her arm beyond the bandages. Then she threw off the covers and stuck her feet out. "Between the toes was a new area of exploitation for me. Easier to ignore the marks when I looked at myself. People don't examine their feet too often.

If you're talking acupuncture, sure, why the hell not. Where's Sabrina?"

"Shower." Joey sat on the edge of the bed and, after twisting off the cap, she handed Carolyn the sports drink. "Drink this. You need to replenish your electrolytes. I wasn't kidding about dehydration."

Carolyn extended a shaky hand and accepted the open drink. Joey helped Carolyn steady the bottle as she took small sips. "If I'd known it was going to be this hard, I think I might have risked the side effects of that weaning drug they recommended. It's a good thing I'm too sick to find a dealer and I don't think I'd survive the look of disappointment in Sabrina's eyes."

"Good, because I don't think I'd survive that either."

Carolyn looked at Joey and seemed like she was about to respond, but took another shaky sip with Joey's assistance before meekly pushing the drink away.

"Now for a few bites of food. I don't expect you to eat it all, but try to get down as much as you can. It will help you."

"Please don't feed me. It's humiliating enough you had to help with the drink. I imagine whatever they put in that sports drink would stain this sweatshirt. I can tell it's one of her favorites."

"It is."

"You're in love with her," Carolyn stated as if this was a well-known fact.

"That looks good." Sabrina's voice interrupted Joey's response to Carolyn's observation.

Sabrina was rubbing her hair dry and had donned a fluffy white robe. "I hope you'll eat a little more than you did last night."

"Already got the fucking lecture. No need to add your stereo two cents," Carolyn barked. "Why don't you and Doctor Do-Good give me a little space? I promise to eat all my veggies like a good girl."

Joey registered the split-second look of hurt on Sabrina's face before she gathered herself to respond. "Okay. Sorry for hovering."

Carolyn sighed. "Perhaps you'll forgive my moodiness. It is one of the side effects of going cold turkey. I'm still trying to figure out why the fuck I chose this route, but I'm halfway there and I'm not about to turn back now and start this shit over. Go."

CHAPTER TEN

Between the bursts of anger, moans of pain, apparent discomfort, and Carolyn's momentary lapses into a severe depressive state, Sabrina was at her wit's end. She no longer believed she was helping. If Joey had a magic formula that would provide even a smidgen of help, she was all for it.

"Please tell me your idea. At this point I would jump up and down, spin around, and say six Hail Mary's backward if I thought it would help." Sabrina rubbed her temples.

Joey grabbed Sabrina's hand and led her to the couch. "Sit. Let me rub your head and I want you to keep an open mind and listen to the whole thing before you comment."

"Okay. I promise. Remember, I'm not beyond chanting something silly at this point." Sabrina sat and took a deep cleansing breath.

"I saw Maribel, and she has a friend."

Sabrina opened her mouth to raise an objection and caught Joey's warning look, then closed her mouth.

Joey grinned. "Good girl, caught yourself. I know Maribel isn't the most reliable source, but I believe she is trying to make up for earlier behavior and, deep within, she has a good heart. Even if we have to dig to China to find it. Her friend is an acupuncturist. She also offered to give you a break. I think Maribel could be good for Carolyn. Sometimes, when there is a vast divide between someone who has royally fucked up and another who is nearly perfect, it's hard for a person to open up. That is especially true when you've had a close relationship in the past. Why do you think the best drug and alcohol counselors are former addicts? They can relate. You can't. I think Maribel can relate to Carolyn. Maybe they can help one another."

"I'm a little worried that Maribel also has the contacts to hook Carolyn up again with drugs. She's very vulnerable now and if she sees an opening or a possibility to score drugs, she'll take it. I'm not sure that's a risk I'm willing to take. I don't trust Maribel."

"You don't trust Carolyn. Maybe you shouldn't, but at some point, she'll be on her own. You can't watch her 24-7 for the next fifty years."

"It's too soon to dangle temptation in front of her."

"Honestly, I think you should give Maribel a chance. Maybe she'll surprise you. Maybe they both will. Self-fulfilling prophecy and all. Assume that Maribel and Carolyn will make you proud and earn that trust, and they will. Presume that they'll both fuck up at the first corner and they'll do that."

Sabrina pushed Joey's shoulder. "Show off. You have to make perfect sense, don't you? Hey, where's that head massage you promised?"

"Turn to your side and I'll let my magic fingers do their thing."

Sabrina swiveled on the couch and Joey massaged her temples. Sabrina tried not to think about those magic hands massaging another part of her body. She felt Joey's hot breath against her neck and wanted to say, *fuck it all*. Maybe Maribel and Joey had it all figured out. Friends with benefits wasn't such a bad thing to consider. They were both adults. As Joey's fingers continued their gentle assault, Sabrina let out an involuntary moan. "God, that feels heavenly."

"Heavenly, huh? Well, you know I could expand my reach."

"Don't tempt me. I'd rather not take a backslide."

Joey stopped massaging her temples and shot Sabrina a quizzical look. "Backslide?"

Sabrina pointedly ignored Joey's question. "You've caught me at a particularly weak moment and I'm counting on your gallantry to not take advantage of the situation. That would be like getting a person shit-faced and then jumping their bones while their inhibitions are taking a vacation."

"Argh. You have to pull the ethics card out. No fair. You tease me by letting me touch you, but not in the way I want. Cruel. That is simply cruel."

Sabrina laughed. "You offered. No woman in their right mind would turn down a head massage or foot rub. Them's the rules. I didn't make them."

"I can see I'm not going to win this debate. So, should I call Maribel and get that acupuncturist here pronto?"

"Yeah, you better go now. Hopefully, we've given Carolyn enough space. I can share the news about some possible relief. Maybe that will keep her from biting off my head again."

†

After making the call to Maribel, Joey returned to the couch to continue massaging Sabrina's temples and then worked her way down to the tensed shoulders. She could feel the knots. She guessed that all of Sabrina's stress settled in her head, neck, and shoulders. Tension headaches were not a lot of fun and neither were pinched nerves in the neck and shoulder region. If a large knot was pushing against a nerve, she was sure that was making Sabrina impatient.

She'd let go the comment about backsliding that had slipped from Sabrina's lips, recognizing her obvious desire not to fill in the blanks. Maybe later Sabrina would come clean. For now, she concentrated on relieving the pressure.

"Relax. Next stop on this tension train is migraineville."

Sabrina sighed. "Already there."

The light knock on the door startled Sabrina. She emerged from the sofa and opened the door to the unknown visitors. The short, muscular woman in a tight T-shirt who accompanied Maribel mildly surprised Joey. Sabrina motioned for them to enter. The woman's short, black, spiked hair was perfectly coiffed as if she was ready to hit the clubs.

"Hi, Maribel. Come on in. The party just started. We're having loads of fun tonight," Sabrina added with a touch of sarcasm. She looked over the new woman. "Hi, I'm Sabrina."

"This is my friend, Bren. She's here to do a treatment on the druggie," Maribel blurted out.

"Shit, Maribel. Do you have to lace everything in bitch, even when doing a good deed?"

"I like her. She doesn't sugarcoat anything. I am a druggie," Carolyn stated. She stood at the edge of the living room with a curious expression on her face. "Let me guess, you're the person about to turn me into a human pincushion"—Carolyn pointed at Bren—"and the other one is my golden ticket to fun. After I kick this shitass habit of mine, I don't suppose a little weed would kill me and I'll bet you can hook me up. Why can't I partake in that? Cancer patients get to toke up when they need a vacation from nausea and the docs are desperate to help them regain weight. It sounds a lot more appealing than needles. That might cause a kind of Pavlov's dog response and I doubt those needles have the same thing I want right about now."

"I don't think taking advantage of our liberal state's laws on marijuana is a good idea." Sabrina pinched the bridge of her nose.

"It's bullshit, you know," Carolyn stated.

"What is?" Joey asked.

"That a little weed is a gateway drug. Maybe if I'd gravitated to that instead of jumping into the hard stuff, I might not be here." Carolyn wobbled and then her pale face erupted in a light sheen of perspiration. She turned back toward the bedroom and mumbled, "I don't think din-din is going to stay where I put it."

Sabrina rushed to help her back to the bedroom and the sound of vomiting punctuated the quiet lull.

"She's had a rough couple of days," Joey apologized.

124

Bren waved her hand in the air. "It's okay. She was more pleasant than a few of my past patients. I get it. I do. I saw enough of it when I was growing up. The biggest risk to her trying to score is managing those cravings. I've had good success, but I won't attempt to bullshit you. A lot of people who try to go cold turkey without medication assistance relapse within weeks or months of getting clean. Often that has fatal consequences because they put too much shit back into their system after it's been clean." Bren shook her head. "It's heartbreaking, really—the number of young folks that OD before their life has even started."

Sabrina arrived in the living room with a panicked look on her face. "She's seizing."

Joey touched her arm before hurrying into the bedroom. By the time she reached Carolyn who had curled herself into a fetal position, it appeared as though the seizure had passed. Joey did a quick assessment and took the vitals she could without her stethoscope and a blood-pressure cuff. Carolyn moaned.

"Carolyn, I think it's time for a return trip to the hospital."

"No, please, I'd rather die than go back. Bring in the acupuncturist. I have a good feeling about that. Convince Sabrina that I'm okay. I'm begging you, Joey."

"All right. We'll give it a try, but if I can't get more food and liquids into you over the next twelve hours, I'm calling the ambulance."

†

Seven days had passed since Carolyn's seizure and she was regaining her health, along with her strength. Sabrina

125

couldn't help but notice her beauty was also slowly returning. Maribel had showed everyone she could be a good friend. Maribel was the only one able to tease out laughter from Carolyn when Sabrina took a short break to walk outside or grab coffee and visit with Joey. She'd return to the apartment and hear the laughter. A part of her was relieved and yet another part of her wondered why she wasn't able to have that same effect.

Sabrina didn't dare have any alcohol or keep any in the apartment. Although alcohol was not Carolyn's drug of choice, Sabrina didn't think replacing one crutch with another was such a grand idea. Joey always offered her wine, but she would refuse, thinking Carolyn might smell it on her breath. She wasn't sure why she cared so much. Maribel didn't. One night she had visited and Sabrina could smell the alcohol leaking from her pores. Before Sabrina left the apartment to get some air, she heard them giggling in the bedroom.

Sabrina was cutting up vegetables for the salad and adding herbs to the salmon. She wanted to cook Carolyn a nice meal and begin a serious discussion about her plans. She wasn't looking forward to the conversation. Although talking with people was her vocation, somehow when she had to use those skills with the people she loved, she felt like she fell short. Emotions got in the way.

After hearing the soft shuffle of Carolyn's slippers across her floor, Sabrina looked up to see Carolyn grinning at her. She continued to pull her hair into a tie and then leaned against the wall watching Sabrina work.

"Hey, can I give you a hand with something? I feel fantastic today. It's about time I pulled my weight around here. I think you should go back to work tomorrow. Not that this place is a pigsty or anything, but it could use a thorough cleaning. After I get everything sparkling like new, maybe I can cook you a meal for once."

Sabrina smiled. "Okay. That sounds like a plan, but leave the laundry."

"Why? You got some kinky attachment to smelly clothes or something?" Carolyn cocked her head.

Sabrina laughed. "Not exactly, but I want to take care of mine and Joey's. A long overdue payback and I want to count how many pairs of underwear Joey has. It wouldn't surprise me if she told me she steals them from her past and present hook ups. The first time we met I counted twenty-six pairs, and that was only a duffel bag worth of laundry. She has three overflowing bags waiting for me. Goodness knows how many are stuffed inside."

"I doubt she's done any hooking up since she met you."

Sabrina ignored Carolyn's observation and wondered if she was redirecting the conversation because she wasn't sure it was true or if she feared that it was. That was a reality she wasn't prepared to unravel for any deeper meaning.

"I thought you wanted to help with dinner. There are potatoes that need dicing. I'm making roasted potatoes with rosemary. You always liked them. Maybe we can talk about things tonight. Like what your long-term plans might be."

"You want me out of your hair, huh? I guess I don't blame you. I haven't been a model guest." Carolyn took several steps to retrieve the bag of red potatoes and cut them in quarters before tossing them into the empty bowl.

"That's not it at all. Look, Carolyn, I know this might be a difficult subject..."

"I get it. We need to talk. I want you to be happy, Sabrina. Are you happy? I mean are you happy with Joey?"

Pushing aside a lock of hair with her forearm, she glanced at Sabrina.

"Joey and I aren't a couple."

"But you want to be, don't you? From my vantage point, she does too."

"It's complicated."

"Don't push her away because you spent most of your formative lesbian years with a fuck up like me. I know you had that short stint on the wild side, but that doesn't count." Carolyn resumed her attack on the potatoes.

"That's not the reason. I'd be a mistress, second to medical school. The timing isn't right. Friendship is good."

"Bullshit. That sexual tension will break one of you, sooner rather than later. Neither of you should let that beast free with someone else. You'll regret it. Trust me on that."

Sabrina set the knife down and turned on the faucet to wash her hands. "Let's talk about something else. You and Maribel seem to get along well..." she began.

"You don't like her, do you?"

"I have my reasons."

"Yeah, she told me. Not everyone can be perfect like you."

"I'm not perfect. Far from it. Don't you remember when we first met?"

"Pftt. You were a baby, then. Every young lesbian I know did that. How else were we going to know who we were sexually compatible with?" Carolyn grinned. "Since then, I'd say you evolved to the very definition of perfection."

"No one is without flaws."

"Tell that to the people who fall madly in love with you. I'll bet Joey would agree." Carolyn finished dicing the last potato and leaned against the counter smiling at Sabrina.

Sabrina laughed. "I seriously doubt that." She flung the hand towel at Carolyn.

"Can you please set the table, while I toss the potatoes in oil and herbs and put them in the oven? Dinner should be ready in about an hour."

"Do we get wine? Don't I deserve a celebratory toast for making it through the week?"

Sabrina frowned. "I don't have any wine. Besides, I don't think that's a great idea. At least not until we get you into an outpatient program and—"

"Fine. No alcohol until I'm able to mimic the Narcotics Anonymous prayer. Although, I never was one to believe in God. Not sure how that will work. It seems disingenuous." Carolyn pulled two plates from the cupboard and then retrieved the silverware from the drawer next to where Sabrina was pouring olive oil into the bowl of diced potatoes.

"A higher power doesn't always mean God. It's a kind of spirituality thing."

"Why can't we all be our own higher power? I can't see myself putting all of my faith in something I can't see, hear, taste, or smell. It feels wrong. Weak. Kinda like I'm absolving myself of all responsibility. How is that taking control of my life? I don't like it. Any feeling of powerlessness kinda irks me. I am not powerless over my addiction. I think I proved that by getting clean without the use of medication."

"Maybe we should find a program that has a different angle. I'll do an Internet search or perhaps Joey knows of something. I doubt the Twelve Step program is the only one out there."

"I sure hope so, because twelve steps seem overly complicated." Carolyn pointed to the open laptop sitting on the coffee table in the living room. "Now I'm curious about those twelve steps. Can I please do a quick search?" Carolyn was already making a beeline toward the computer.

"Sure, we have time before dinner is ready. Um, do you mind if I call Joey and invite her to dinner? She's been a rock to me and super sweet to you. It'd be a nice way to thank her. Don't you think?" Sabrina knew she was taking the easy way out of having that serious discussion. When she broached the topic of Carolyn's long-term plans, it would be a bonus to have Joey's steady presence. She could step in if things went sideways.

Carolyn seemed absorbed in her search and absently waved her hand. "Sure, whatever." She glanced up. "Maybe you can invite Maribel too. She's been just as much of a help to both of us. I only put two place settings on the table."

"That's okay, I'll grab two more after I finish with the potatoes." Shit, I guess that discussion will have to move to the back burner now. Damn, where's that bottle of wine when I need it.

Sabrina finished spreading the seasoned potatoes onto the foil sitting on top of a cookie sheet she'd laid aside. After popping the red potatoes into the oven, she retrieved two more place settings and added them to the table. A second or two passed before she ambled to the couch and relaxed against the cushions. She was mentally going over what else she needed to prepare for dinner and almost forgot the most important item—calling Joey to invite her over. She also needed to make her way to Maribel's apartment since she didn't have her cell programmed into her own smartphone. Sabrina watched Carolyn scrolling through a website reading the screen and frowning. Believing this was a good time to call, she grabbed her phone. She pushed up from the couch and punched in the numbers.

"Hey you. Wanna come to dinner? I'm making something disgustingly healthy... Salmon, roasted red potatoes, grilled asparagus and a nice salad... Great. Oh, hey, if you see Maribel in the hallway or have a chance to swing by her place, can you invite her as well? Thanks... In about an hour. Oh, and bring that mound of smelly clothes. I will definitely tackle that tonight." Sabrina set her phone back on top of the counter and joined Carolyn who appeared to be waiting for her to return.

"There is no fucking way I'm doing the Twelve Step program. They mention God in seven of the twelve steps." Carolyn wrinkled her nose. "And the first step is admitting my powerlessness, which I completely disagree with."

"Okay, the Twelve Step program is out. There have to be other options."

Carolyn smiled. "There are. I can still hang with other druggies and get the support I need through a group. None of that powerlessness shit exists with this program called SMART recovery. The emphasis is on motivation, personal responsibility, and balance. I don't see any of that 'it's out of my control shit where I blame an unknown force.' I'm the one who fucked up, so I'm the one who needs to take responsibility, not lay the blame somewhere else."

Sabrina draped her arm over Carolyn's shoulder and leaned into her. "I'm proud of you. You know that?"

Carolyn scrunched her face in disbelief. "You are?"

"Yes, I am. Don't be so surprised. You showed the kind of fortitude that few, including me, possess. I have one tiny suggestion."

"Oh no, here it comes."

"Not many people in recovery survive without the considerable support of others and while I think this SMART recovery program might be a great fit for you, perhaps an independent counselor is something to consider."

"I can't afford counseling. I don't have money for that. I don't even have a job yet. I already have a considerable amount of guilt over mooching off you." Carolyn leaned forward with her head in her hands.

"A good friend cannot ever mooch off someone else. The world is always a better place whenever we can pay it forward and help someone in their time of need. We'll work it out. You can pay me back when you get on your feet if that makes you feel any better. Please let me do this for you. I wasn't there for you when you needed me. I have a vested interest in your full recovery because I do not want to go through this cold turkey thing again with you. I can only take so much abuse when bitchy Carolyn comes out to play."

Carolyn chuckled. "I was a bitch, wasn't I?"

Sabrina nodded. "I knew what I was getting into. It was all part of the process. Being sick is no fun. You get a pass."

CHAPTER ELEVEN

Sabrina was determined to have a few precious hours to herself. She enjoyed Joey's company, but in the last week, she hadn't taken much time to relax and reflect on her life. Even when Maribel came over, she was hesitant to leave her with Carolyn for too long. Sabrina was still leery about her influence over someone so fragile.

Joey had offered to keep her company while she tackled the massive amount of laundry, but she had staunchly refused. She'd insisted that a few hours to herself were critical to her sanity. Sabrina needed the breathing room with nothing to do but read a good book and veg while waiting for the telltale dings from the machines. She hadn't articulated her hesitancy about leaving Maribel alone with Carolyn, but she knew and so did Carolyn that she had to trust both of them sometime. Carolyn wasn't stupid and the look on her face said it all. Carolyn needed a sign from Sabrina acknowledging her faith in Carolyn's ability to stay on the path of recovery. Sabrina vowed to herself that she would wring Maribel's neck if she did anything to wave temptation in front of Carolyn's nose. So far Maribel had stayed well within the boundaries. When she hadn't brought wine to dinner, Sabrina felt a huge sense of relief. After she opened the door, she was half expecting Maribel to have some kind of alcohol in her hand. Maribel had grinned and handed her a bottle of non-alcoholic sparkling cider. Joey had done the same.

Sabrina was giggling as she counted out the pairs of underwear and noted with some suspicion that a few of them were not quite what she expected Joey might wear. *Forty-two. Holy shit. Who has forty-two pairs of underwear?* She wondered for the second time if she could get away with nicking one of the pairs she'd coveted before. Stealing a pair of Joey's underwear was almost becoming a compulsion as she handled each pair—tantalizingly warm, straight from the dryer. She held up a skimpy thong and thought Joey would not be caught dead in this type of lingerie. She twirled the thong in her fingers and then she heard someone clear their throat.

"Ahem. I see you're entertaining yourself again with my undergarments. I'm not going to admit where I procured that little gem. Unfortunately, desperate times call for desperate measures and a scarcity of clean underwear forced me to wear that uncomfortable piece of fabric. I only have a few pairs of jeans, so the option of commando was out. I found it in my special drawer. I used to have a quirk shall we say.

Yeah, let's call it a quirk. I'd almost forgotten about my stash until my only choice was to raid that corner of my closet."

"I'm not sure I want to know the story. Until now I assumed you were a normal, well-adjusted person." Sabrina placed the thong on top of the other laundry.

"In my defense, my, um, former partners inadvertently left the first few pairs behind. After that, superstition took over any amount of sanity I had before my habit took root." Joey grinned. "Now I can't help myself."

"Are you serious?"

"As a heart attack."

"I'm almost afraid to ask." She handed Joey two bags stuffed with clean clothes and then picked up the third and placed it on top of her basket. "But I think I have to know the full story."

Joey cringed. "I'm afraid of what you'll think of me. It isn't as bad as it might sound."

"Do you think Maribel and Carolyn will be okay on their own, because I have to hear this?" Sabrina was laughing now as she headed for the exit to the laundry room. "Come on, I'm dying for a glass of wine and a good story."

"Fine, but don't forget I warned you."

†

Joey was second guessing her earlier confession as they entered her apartment toting her fresh laundry. Sabrina had dropped off her own basket and checked on Maribel and Carolyn. She was thankful for the growing friendship between Sabrina's ex and her sometimes reckless friend. Although there was a chance the two would be a horrible influence on one another, Joey believed there was an equal chance for the opposite.

What if Sabrina thinks I'm completely off my rocker?

Sabrina brushed her fingers against Joey's arm. "Hey, get that panicked look off your face. You don't have to reveal any deep dark secrets if you don't want to. I promise I won't think any less of you, no matter what you tell me. Everyone has secrets, remember? I believe I've gotten to know you well enough over the past several weeks to form an impression. I'm very good at my job and I can see through bullshit, you know. I've seen the real you."

"Sit, while I get you some wine and deposit my clothes into the bedroom. I'll put them away later."

"Ooh, I'll put your clothes away for you. It will give me a chance to check out that secret stash of yours. I'm dying to know how many pairs of panties you own," Sabrina teased.

"Ha ha, you're a real comedian. Sit and behave."

Making her way to the couch, Sabrina sprawled out with her arm resting on one of the throw pillows as Joey tossed her laundry into the other room. She grabbed a bottle of wine and made quick work of removing the cork.

Setting the two empty glasses on the coffee table along with the full bottle, Joey sat and began. "I can't believe I'm going to tell you all this. You need to remember that when this started, I was young."

"I can't wait to hear the story. This sounds juicy. I have my own youthful indiscretions."

Pouring the wine into the glasses, Joey continued, "I want to hear about those, but I'll show you mine first. So, um, the first time I had, uh, sex with a woman, I was in my senior year of high school. We were two kids who didn't know what the hell we were doing and Stacy's panties kind of got pushed to the bottom of the bed. When my father almost caught us, she quickly dressed leaving them where they'd ended up after our fumbling night of passion. I was going to give them back when I found them the next day after stripping the bed, but she joked that I should keep them as a reminder. So I did."

"Okay, that doesn't sound weird at all."

"I haven't told the whole story yet." Joey lifted her glass to her lips and took a big gulp. "At the time of this first acquisition—that's what I call my quirk—I was wearing boxers. They don't work well with all styles of clothing. When I wore a snug pair of jeans, I'd absently tug on my boxers to keep them from bunching up. I was on a quest for the perfect underwear."

Sabrina sipped on her wine. "Boy, can I relate to that."

"I know, right? I took years to find the answer. Anyway, I thought, what the hell, maybe I should try on Stacy's panties and see if they were better. And that's where my obsession took root and became a full-blown monster after Stacey and I parted ways. College was a crazy time. Lots of women and lots of panties. I had a certain type. I chose women of the more feminine variety. Those types usually wore the frillier styles. Thus, I did not find a more comfortable pair."

Sabrina's face scrunched in confusion. "Um, I think you might be leaving out a few details. How did you manage to, um, acquire these panties? I can imagine you had the skill to charm a number of women out of their panties, but surely most of them would want them back?"

Joey stood and paced. "That's the part that will have you running for the hills and far away from me. In the beginning, I would get up in the middle of the night to pee or something and then find a way to hide them without my date catching me. Kicking them under the dresser usually worked, but occasionally I had to get creative."

"You stole their panties?" Sabrina laughed.

Joey was perplexed with Sabrina's response. She became more confident in telling the story as she realized that maybe Sabrina wouldn't judge her too harshly after all. "At the time I had convinced myself I was only borrowing them. I wanted to wash them, try them on, wash them again, and then I planned on giving them back."

"What happened to that original plan?"

"Well, there isn't really one answer." Joey cringed. "Most of the time, I wouldn't know the women well enough to find them again. On other occasions, the timing was all off because I wouldn't run across them for weeks or months. I didn't think saying to them, in the middle of the quad, 'oh hey, come on back to my room tonight, I have your panties' would elicit a warm reception." Joey paused and stood up. She paced the room.

"Spit it out. There is more, isn't there?"

"I continued my quest for the perfect panty and one day I picked up this woman who was not my type at all. She was on the butch side, but very, very sexy. Anyway, she was wearing a pair of boi shorts and I was so eager to steal those undies, she almost caught me. I scooped them up and took them into the bathroom then tossed them into the cabinet right before I heard her stirring in the other room. The next morning when she asked if I'd seen her underwear, I almost confessed. She said they were her lucky shorts, and she hated to lose them. I promised I would get them back to her when I found them. I never break a promise, but I was also eager to give the boi shorts a try. I vowed to test them out and then I

138

would call her up and return them to her. This is where superstition enters the story."

"Wow, I can't wait to hear this part, because, you know, it isn't at all strange up to now," Sabrina joked.

Sabrina's mirthful response to her story soothed Joey, and she continued. "I returned her boi shorts after I'd worn them. I'd found the perfect pair of underwear. But the minute I returned her boi shorts, a series of unfortunate events occurred. I received my first B on a test. Playing a game of pickup volleyball, I suffered a very painful sprain. And finally, I lost the ring my mother gave me for my thirteenth birthday. I decided right then and there, I could never give back the underwear I stole, ever again. I convinced myself that bad things would happen. Since then, I never have. I am a blatant panty thief. In my defense, I always shove a couple of twenties in their purses or pockets to cover the cost of my theft."

Sabrina bent over laughing. "You know the answer to your kleptomania is to get yourself in a real relationship and then you'll never have to resort to a life of crime ever again."

"True, I didn't steal panties when I was in my committed relationship."

"I must admit, it sounds decadent to steal panties from some unsuspecting woman. So naughty. I will admit that I covet those boi shorts of yours with the covers on them. I entertained the idea of nicking one. Now I am especially tempted because of your explanation that boi shorts are the perfect panty."

Joey chuckled and returned to the couch. "I'd recommend stealing a pair without the covers because I'd probably never miss a plain one."

"Duly noted." Sabrina's face adopted a serious expression. "You've never been caught?"

Joey shook her head.

"You know you have to stop, right? I mean, superstition aside, it seems like you harbor a bit of guilt over your illegal escapades. I know these thefts aren't significant but they seem to affect you. It's like any addiction, when it leaks into your life in unproductive ways, it's time to stop."

"Well, like you said, when I find the right woman, it will stop." Joey nodded her head and returned to the couch. "Time for you to confess now. Don't think for a minute I would let those comments about backsliding or youthful indiscretions go unexplored."

"Right, I guess that's a fair request. You metaphorically showed me yours and now I need to show mine. Before I met Carolyn, I was a lot more like you. I'm not saying it was bad or anything. Really, Joey, I have no judgement about your philosophy regarding having friends with benefits. It's just that having a string of one-night stands stopped being right for me, especially after I met Carolyn. It didn't fit who I am. When I first discovered I liked girls, I wanted to experience that whole new world. And I did. I will not admit to how many women I slept with. Suffice to say it was a lot by any person's standards."

"Okay, wow. That was not what I expected. Too bad I didn't know you then."

Sabrina backhanded Joey. "I'm never confessing anything to you ever again."

"Sorry, sorry. Hey, for what it's worth, I don't at all think any less of you. In fact, you've just ratcheted up a notch in my perfection meter."

Sabrina laughed. "Perfection meter? That seems counterintuitive. Perfection by its very definition would not exist on a meter."

"As you've learned I have a unique view of life. New topic, now that we've bared our souls to one another. What are you going to do about Carolyn? Does she have plans?"

"Good question. I was going to talk to her about that tonight and then I kind of chickened out and invited you and Maribel to join us."

"I was wondering about that. Especially the part about Maribel joining us. I know she isn't your favorite person, but she has been a model friend to Carolyn. I think she could be good for her and vice versa. Not that we aren't all damaged in some way, but the two of them seem damaged in ways that maybe only they can truly understand. You know?"

"I don't trust her."

"Yeah, I get that. But you cannot control the mistakes people choose to make on their own. Temptation presents itself to all of us every single day. It's different for each of us. Falling down isn't always a bad thing. Sometimes life's lessons are harsh, and we need someone to help us up, and other times, we have to do it on our own. You can't be there for her every single minute to guarantee she makes the choices you believe are best for her. Give her space to fly on her own. Do you think you'll get back together with her? Clearly there is still love between the two of you. I'm not blind to that."

"No." Sabrina vigorously shook her head. "Our time has passed. Yes, I still love her, but I don't think the tear in our relationship can ever be repaired. What you said is correct, she needs to venture on her own without me. I think getting back together would be the absolute worst thing for her in her recovery. It wouldn't be good for me either. I believe there is this co-dependent thing that's hard for us to break. Not that I think therapy is a bad thing, obviously. I don't have the time or energy to do a lot of work on myself. I know I have a tendency to swoop in and save someone to the point of unhealthy co-dependency. I'd rather find someone stable."

"Damn. I think I've just lost my chance with you, then. You know, after my recent confession to being a panty thief."

Sabrina pushed against Joey's shoulder. "Nah, it has nothing to do with that and everything to do with your primary relationship—medical school."

"I won't be in medical school forever."

"True dat." Sabrina smiled.

Joey let the response pass and wondered if her insistence on remaining single would last. Every day her feelings for Sabrina increased. This temptation was far greater than the one she had for collecting underwear.

CHAPTER TWELVE

Nearly a month had passed and Sabrina knew it was a bad idea to continue sleeping next to Carolyn. There was no reason for it. Carolyn was healthy enough not to need Sabrina by her side. Citing that her apartment only had one bedroom, and they were both adults, sounded flimsy to her own ears. She could imagine how that might land on Joey. *Joey. What would she think?* Sabrina knew she didn't owe Joey any explanation. They weren't in a committed relationship. They weren't even in a casual one. And yet she felt like she needed to explain this to her.

As Carolyn lay in her arms, Sabrina couldn't help how the feelings stirred in her. She didn't want her arousal to rear its ugly head. Every day Carolyn's beauty returned a little more and Sabrina was only human. She slipped out from under Carolyn's embrace as she continued to sleep peacefully. There was a kind of comfort in returning to how they used to be. And yet, this felt wrong. Oh, so wrong. Sabrina gathered her strength to have the conversation tonight after she returned from the clinic. She also needed to resume writing her dissertation. The month with Carolyn had demanded all her focus and energy. She'd fallen behind on the timeline she'd laid out for herself. It was too late to change topics now. Her theory on the fifth pane would have to end up on the cutting room floor. She didn't have the time to devote to it.

As Sabrina finished buttoning her blouse, she heard Carolyn stir. She stretched and then repositioned herself in the bed. Sabrina noted with relief that Carolyn was regaining some of her curves as her T-shirt lifted slightly above her midriff to expose her middle. She was still thin, but evidence of a healthier diet was making its presence known.

"You look nice. What time will you be back tonight?"

"I should be back by five."

"Okay, I'll have dinner ready. I'm looking forward to cooking for you. It was the one thing I used to do well. Or at least I thought so unless you were lying to me all those years."

Sabrina chuckled. "No, you're a fantastic cook. Inventive sometimes with the ingredients you chose to put together, but rarely did I object. Um, can it just be the two of us tonight?"

The line between Carolyn's forehead appeared. "Of course. I guess we're going to have a serious discussion then."

"Don't be alarmed. I'm not tossing you out or anything drastic like that."

"I know. You wouldn't ever do that. You're one of the good guys. That will never change. It's why I love you so much."

Sabrina frowned. "Everything will be okay. I promise. Look, I've got to go or I'll be late. They were very kind to give me so much time off and I don't want to press my luck."

"Sure, go. You should have woken me earlier and I could have made breakfast, or at least had coffee ready for you."

"I can grab a muffin and latte on the way. It isn't that hard to find in the coffee capital of the US."

"So I've noticed. Have a great day."

Sabrina gave Carolyn a small wave and exited. The stress of the situation and her feelings for Carolyn swirled around in her stomach. She wondered if coffee on an empty stomach was such a wise idea. But then the caffeine withdrawal and a likely headache wasn't very appealing either. Joey would chastise her for having a sugary muffin with empty calories rather than something healthier that would absorb the acid in the coffee. Sabrina wondered if Joey had left for her ED rotation yet. Maybe she would pass her in the hall on the way to her clerkship.

†

Joey was happy to bump into Sabrina on her way to her clinical rotation but recognized something was wrong right away. "Hey, you okay?"

"Yeah," Sabrina added absently.

"Want me to cook for you or bring takeover tonight, because you know I can only cook one thing. And, I don't do that one thing all that well."

145

"No, I'm finally having the talk tonight with Carolyn. It's way overdue," Sabrina answered. "Rain check?"

"Of course. If you want to come over later, we can dissect the whole conversation. I'll take a break and be a good friend. You don't need a special invite you know. Stop by anytime. Day or night." Joey slung her arm over Sabrina and squeezed.

"Thanks. I may need an outside perspective. So, yeah, I'll take you up on your generous offer. I'll admit to feeling conflicted right now."

Joey nodded. "I can relate. Conflicted is a good word. Hey, sorry I have to dash if I'm gonna catch my bus."

"Yeah, me too. I have to hurry if I'm going to arrive on time."

The bus bumped along as Joey stuck her headphones into her ears. This quiet time before her shift was important to Joey. Listening to music and tuning out the rest of the world was a habit that allowed her to center herself. It was an alternative form of meditation in her mind. Although Seattle was a clean city, she'd still caught a whiff of the diesel fumes from some big truck and the blaring horns from several impatient drivers. Those small invasions into her senses had put her off kilter.

Her thoughts kept returning to Sabrina's pained expression this morning. She'd mentioned confusion and that worried Joey. *What if she gets back together with Carolyn?* Although Sabrina had categorically denied that would happen, Joey had her doubts. If Sabrina wasn't able to achieve closure for both, the feelings would linger and temptation would override any logical thought process. Joey believed logic and restraint were overrated. She wanted to begin a relationship with Sabrina. She'd admitted that to herself this morning as she got ready. She'd almost convinced herself to throw caution to the wind and broach the subject with Sabrina. After all, weren't they already in a relationship, sans the sex? She spent all of her free time with Sabrina. Surely she could juggle everything and maintain something solid and healthy.

Fortunately, Joey opened her eyes just in time to realize the bus had reached her stop. Leaving her seat, she gave a small wave to the bus driver before exiting. She wanted to have a busy day in the ED. That would be the only way to keep her brain from obsessing over what to do with Sabrina.

A steady flow of patients made their way through the ED and soon it was lunchtime. On her way to the cafeteria, Joey was surprised to see Maribel waiting for her as she walked down the corridor. Maribel was leaning against the wall.

"Hey, do you have time to talk?" Maribel asked.

Joey thought she looked a little lost and vulnerable as she pushed away from the wall.

"Sure, but I only have thirty minutes. If this is going to take longer than that, maybe you can come by tonight for dinner."

"You aren't hanging with Sabrina tonight?"

"No, she wants to spend the time alone with Carolyn."

"Oh, I see. Well, I guess that answers that. Never mind—"

"Hey, wait." Joey grabbed Maribel's arm. "Come on, I have a few minutes to kill and then we can finish up tonight. Tell me what's up, please? Go find us a table and I'll get us some healthy food."

She had to admit she cared for Maribel. Sometimes Maribel dropped the facade and Joey liked that person, but she would never be in love with her. Joey realized that

147

compared to Sabrina, no one would stack up to her. Joey had to be careful to show she cared enough for their friendship to listen, but not lead her on.

"Try to find something that will taste good, okay?"

After bringing the salads and water to the table, Joey asked, "So what's on your mind?"

"I'd like to ask Carolyn to go on a date." Maribel held out her hand. "I know, probably the stupidest idea I've ever had. I don't date. She's still in love with her ex. Not to mention a brand-new recruit to the whole clean and sober life."

"It's not the stupidest idea."

"It's not?"

"No, I think you two might be good for each other, but I would suggest you tread lightly. Carolyn's shit is not all together quite yet. I think any kind of serious relationship is far down the road for her."

"Well, that's not a problem for me. I'm not looking for serious right now either. Do you think Sabrina and Carolyn will get back together?" Maribel asked.

"I honestly don't know the answer to that question. I wish I did. I think they both still love each other. Sabrina insists that boat has sailed, but I'm not so sure."

"You should tell her."

"Tell her what?" Joey paused before taking a sip of her water.

"Don't be obtuse. You are like the most intelligent person I know."

Joey dragged her fingers through her hair. "Damn. No, definitely not. She's got some unfinished business with Carolyn to resolve. I guess my advice to you is don't pursue anything other than friendship until you're sure you know which direction the wind is gonna blow."

"Well, I do the friends with benefits thing extremely well."

"Not with benefits, Maribel. For once, temper that impetuous side. If you want a serious shot at dating Carolyn, take the necessary time to nurture something—even if neither of you are ready to walk down the aisle."

"Aw, you are no fun anymore since you fell in love."

"You'll be joining me in boringville soon. I can already tell. I give you two years, max." Joey grinned.

†

Sabrina noticed the light application of eye makeup on Carolyn and braced herself for an interesting night. Her eyes shifted to the lighted candles and beautifully set table.

"This looks nice."

"Thanks, give me a second. Dinner is almost done. I didn't find a lot to work with, so it isn't fancy, but I think it's edible." Carolyn's eyes twinkled.

"I'm sure it'll be wonderful. You look beautiful tonight."

Sabrina wished she hadn't added that last part. That would not help with what she had to tell Carolyn. She'd move out to the couch and let Carolyn have her bed for as long as she needed to stay. If she ended up sleeping with Carolyn after all the time they were apart, she knew it would be for all the wrong reasons. All day long she had thought about Carolyn and Joey. She'd admitted to herself that if she had sex with Carolyn, she would wish it was Joey and that wasn't fair to Carolyn.

Carolyn gave Sabrina a side glance. "Thanks. Hey, don't look so worried. I won't read anything more into it than a compliment. I won't deny hearing that felt good, and something I need right about now, but I'm not holding my breath for—you know."

"I don't want to hurt you. That's the last thing I desire to have happen."

"I know. I put on makeup for me, mostly. It was a way to feel good about myself. My therapist helped me think of ways to do that. Sit. We will have a nice dinner, get everything out in the open, and then I promise the sun will rise again tomorrow."

Sabrina set her bag on the counter and then asked, "I can't help with anything?"

"Nope. Everything is almost ready."

"Okay. It looks fabulous and so healthy. Joey must have rubbed off on you." Sabrina fidgeted at the table while she waited for Carolyn to add the sliced chicken to the rainbow-colored salad.

Carolyn laid the two salads on the table and gestured for Sabrina to eat. "You already know there wasn't any wine to add to this offering, but bon appetite."

After taking a small bite of the salad, Sabrina racked her brain for a way to start the conversation. "So, besides cooking this fabulous meal"—she swiveled her head around to check out the apartment—"and probably using a toothbrush to clean every single corner of the place, did you do anything else interesting today?"

"As a matter of fact, I did. I went looking for work."

"So, you've decided to stay in Seattle."

"Yeah, only if that's okay with you. I've got nothing to return to back home and I've already made other friends. Thanks to you. Maribel and Joey are cool."

"Seattle can be a very expensive place to live. I'm barely making it. I should have gotten a roommate instead of a one-bedroom apartment. I would have rented a studio, but nothing was available. I'll be paying off my student loans for the rest of my natural life."

Carolyn frowned. "You don't want me to stay?"

"That's not what I said." Sabrina reached out and clasped Carolyn's hand, giving her a light squeeze.

"Once I start my job, I can help with the bills. I may be many things, but when we were together, I always pulled my weight."

"I know that. This is a one bedroom, Carolyn. I was going to tell you it's a good idea for me to move out to the couch until you get back on your feet."

"Don't be ridiculous, I'll crash on the couch. This is your apartment. I can look for a place as soon as I save up some money. Or, we could get either a pullout bed or futon and we can help each other out. I literally have nothing to move into this small space. And the limited amount of clothing I'll be able to afford to buy could fit in a tiny suitcase that I can stuff in a closet."

"Wait, you have a job already?"

"Yeah, Maribel hooked me up with this hippie chick who works at an upscale coffee place. They needed someone right away because this other person walked off the job without notice. I'll be their new barista. It isn't much, but it will help pay the bills. I also looked into culinary school. I think I'd like to learn to be a chef."

"Wow, Carolyn. I don't know quite what to say. You always were someone who, once you set your sights on something did not let the grass grow under your feet. I am so proud of you."

"I'm gonna do right by you this time around, I promise. I know we can't turn back time and return to the way things were..."

"One day at a time. We'll take things one day at a time. But, Carolyn, just friendship, okay? Sex has a way of messing things up."

"I know, I know. Sex was another addiction for me and I have a ways to go to slay that dragon."

"Be careful with Maribel. I can't tell you what to do, but Maribel has a rather carefree attitude about sex."

"Yeah, I know that too. We talked about it. We're just friends. At this point, friends is more important as a way to get back on my feet. Rather adult of me to have that perspective so soon, huh?"

"Shockingly so. Trust me, I see tons of people struggle with all kinds of issues and I don't think I've ever seen this level of commitment to change in such a short time."

"I had nowhere else to go but up. I also found places in Seattle for the SMART Recovery meetings. I'm gonna check them out. Have I mentioned how much I love the Internet?" Carolyn smiled.

"Yeah, that is a modern marvel. I don't admit this to my professors, but a good deal of information embedded into my dissertation came from the Internet."

"Look, Sabrina, I know you aren't the judgmental type, but you also shouldn't become concerned if Maribel and I venture into a different phase. You and I didn't think all that differently about sex at one time. I know you can understand that sometimes, Sabrina, there is nothing wrong with having sex without being in love, as long as the boundaries of that relationship are clear. I get that this perspective is more dangerous for someone with an addictive personality, and I'm working through all the complicated ramifications of that with my therapist, so don't worry."

"I'll try to keep that in mind and not jump to the conclusion that your future choices aren't healthy for you."

Carolyn's beauty once again entranced Sabrina. Sitting next to her was the woman she had fallen in love with. Even so, a tiny niggling feeling inside left the door open to considering if it was possible to turn back time and try again.

Sabrina shifted the conversation back to her original purpose for talking with Carolyn. "Maybe we can look for something that won't kill your back this weekend. Futons have come a long way over the years. I remember the one my mother brought home was terrible, but that was so long ago. I think that would be better than one of those blow-up beds because we could turn it into a couch each morning. Seattle also has a fair number of second-hand stores with decent clothing if you don't mind shopping there. I get all my clothes from the consignment shops. Women are so fickle, especially the rich Seattlites, and they often dump off perfectly good clothes. You can, of course, borrow my clothes any time you want. I don't have a huge wardrobe, but they're clean and comfortable."

Carolyn leaned in and kissed Sabrina on the cheek. "Thanks."

†

"Can I ask you something?" Maribel looked intently at Joey as they relaxed on the couch.

"Sure."

"Do you think it's possible for someone to change? You know, really change. Like fundamentally who they've been."

"Hmm. That's a great question. Brings into play the whole uncertainty of nature versus nurture, but from a different perspective. I believe this requires wine, and then we can thoroughly explore that topic. I must say, I didn't realize you had the capacity for such depth."

Maribel shoved Joey's shoulder. "Asshole."

As Joey was pouring the wine she continued, "Sabrina and I have talked about facades and how we all have them and present those to the world. It isn't about hiding certain parts of ourselves from others and even ourselves, it's more about trying to show yourself in the best light. Maybe fundamental changes aren't what's happening. Maybe when people change, all they are doing is uncovering that part of themselves that nobody has seen before, not even themselves."

"Well, that doesn't make sense. Why would I present a total bitch facade? Surely that isn't trying to trick others into seeing my best side." Maribel sipped her wine.

"Humans are complicated beings. Intent and motivation are sometimes hard to understand. Forget trying to understand someone else, even the shrinks don't do that well. I also don't believe anyone has such a great grasp on understanding their own motivations. Maybe it's because we don't want to face the cold hard truth. Maybe it's a defense mechanism. I'm not sure. I'm a hard science person. I deal in facts and data. Evidence. Understanding the psyche is messy."

Maribel shrugged. "Yeah, I guess."

Joey placed her hand on top of Maribel's thigh. "Maribel, you're a good person. My advice is not to change to find that inner good for anyone but yourself."

"You know, I admire Carolyn. She's doing something. It's gotta be hard to crawl out from the place she's been, but she already has a job and a plan to stay clean and sober."

"She does?" Joey asked.

"Yeah, I hooked her up with Darci at the Morning Drip. They needed a barista and Carolyn needed a job. I thought it was the perfect match. Darci's cool. She understands what Carolyn is going through. Slayed her own dragon three years ago. I think she feels the need to pay it forward."

Joey's heart was pounding. A part of her wanted good things for Carolyn, and yet she worried that with each step forward, her chance with Sabrina was slipping away. If Carolyn could change and turn her life around, then what would stop Sabrina and Carolyn from becoming a couple again? This was a conundrum Joey wasn't prepared to face at this time. Maybe she needed to do a bit of changing as well. If she did, was she ignoring her own advice to Maribel about not changing for someone else? Besides, what would she change? Her singular focus on school at the expense of everything else in her life, including love?

Maribel touched Joey's arm. "Hey, where did you go just now?"

Joey shook her head. "Oh, I was thinking about change. Yeah, not only can all of us change if we want, we do it without acknowledging that change. You won't be the same person you are now in ten years, twenty years. That's not a good or bad thing. I was wondering about how fast that change is gonna come for me and if, in the meantime, I'll miss out because I'm stuck in a stage."

Maribel laughed. "You mean your insistence to spend all your free time studying and missing out on life? Yeah, you better go after Sabrina before she slips away. I'm only saying this so the avenue is clear for me. Because, fuck that I'm a good person shit. I'm not." Maribel opened her arms and pointed at herself. "What you see is what you get."

"I seriously doubt that. In this case, raging waters run deep. You're already changing and you haven't figured that out yet."

"So are you, my sexy ex fuck buddy, so are you."

CHAPTER THIRTEEN

"I'm taking a break from studies. A whole weekend where I vow not to crack open a book or sneak into my kindle," Joey blurted out. She stretched out with a thick textbook on her lap and made the comment without looking up.

Sabrina turned her attention to Joey and wondered where this was coming from. She hadn't asked about the new futon or the sleeping arrangements, but the other day when Joey had come to her apartment, Sabrina had watched as her eyes traveled to the new piece of furniture and a broad smile had danced across her face.

"Really? And what are you planning for this lost weekend?"

"A trip to Forks. Come with me. You promised to take the trip with me and see where I've committed myself to live for three frickin' years after medical school."

"All you have to do is cue up the *Twilight* series. The answers are all there. You don't have to waste a weekend to get a feel for the place," Sabrina joked.

"*Au contraire.* And I want you with me when I experience it for the first time."

"What? Please tell me you did not sign a contract without spending time there?" Sabrina set aside her laptop and studied Joey.

Joey made a face. "The offer was generous. It was hard to refuse."

"Okay, but it's like four hours from civilization. And, I thought you didn't have a car," Sabrina argued.

"I'm borrowing a friend's."

Sabrina quirked her eyebrow. "A friend? You could have asked me. Sure, my car's a beater, but I think it would make it to Forks."

"No offense, but my friend's vehicle is a lot nicer. He's one of the ED docs I work with. He's like sixty, so don't make any assumptions. Are you up for a road trip or not?"

"Sure, why the hell not? Do I get to bring my laptop? I still have edits to do on my dissertation. I'm trying to make up for lost time." When Sabrina looked at Joey's crestfallen face she hurried to add, "Or not. How about I jump in that cold lake with you and we'll make this a weekend for fun and fun alone? No work. Okay?" The brilliant smile that returned to Joey's face made it all worthwhile to delay the submission of her dissertation. Her professor had given her a little wiggle room after she'd been honest about how the month she'd helped Carolyn had put her behind.

Rescheduling the meeting would not be a huge problem and this weekend seemed important to Joey.

Joey grinned as she explained. "I got the hospital to spring for accommodations while we check out the area."

"I thought you were going to work at a clinic."

"The hospital owns the clinic and an outpatient behavioral health program. I might have mentioned that I would ask my friend who is currently finishing up her PhD program. If you're interested in learning more about the behavioral health clinic, I have a number for someone eager to meet you."

"Oh really?"

"You never know when opportunity decides to knock on your door. Keep an open mind. Oh, and guess what?"

"I'm sure I don't know what other surprises you have up your sleeve."

Joey smirked. "Remember that author friend who gave me those special panties?"

"Yeah."

"Well, she lives in Forks and we're supposed to hook up?"

"Please, don't tell me she's another one of your former stress relievers."

"God, no. She's happily married and could be my mother. I can distract her while you rummage through her home so you can steal a pair of panties."

"Hardy, har, har."

"Admit it. Ever since you heard my story, you've been dying to walk on the wild side. And, since you don't do one-night stands anymore, your only chance to nick a pair of panties will be with my friend. She has loads. I think she made up a bunch as a joke and didn't give them all out at the last writers' conference she went to. I doubt she'll miss a pair. I promise."

"You, Joey Hartford, are a terrible influence on me."

"This is going to be a weekend you'll never forget. I promise."

"Maybe, but will it be for very good or very bad reasons? If I end up wearing orange and having to join a prison gang, I'll never forgive you."

"So dramatic. I'm sure stealing one pair of panties is considered a misdemeanor. Theft in like the hundredth degree or something. And just so you know, the levels work in the opposite direction, the higher the number, the less the crime is."

"When is this little crime spree weekend supposed to begin?" Sabrina asked.

"Be ready to leave at noon on Friday. Seattle traffic is a bitch, you know, so if we don't leave by noon it will take us eight hours to get there versus four."

"That means I'll need to ask my boss to let me leave early and rearrange my afternoon appointments." Sabrina frowned. "I'm not sure I have the credits yet to ask for more time off so soon after my month of intermittent time away from the clinic."

"Psht, I'll bet you didn't take off a single minute, prior to helping out Carolyn. Want me to call him?" Joey set the thick textbook to the side.

"Her, and no thanks."

"Her, hmm. Is she cute? A lesbian?"

"No, and no. Wait, I don't mean she's unattractive, just older and not my type. God, I can't believe we're talking about my boss and physical attractiveness like two shallow high school girls." Sabrina sighed.

"Can you please ask her, otherwise we'll have to leave at the ass crack of dawn."

"Fine, she'll undoubtedly say yes, because she's just that nice. I'm the one who will feel like crap for asking."

"You are way too responsible for your own good," Joey said.

"Hello pot, kettle here. I'm calling you out."

"And that is exactly why we both need this weekend. We must make a solemn oath to one another to ensure this is a weekend of complete debauchery in every single way. We'll drink too much, party too much, steal a few pairs of panties, and exit town wondering what the hell hurricane blew through, leaving them in awe of our brilliance." Joey grinned.

"I don't believe hurricanes leave anything but destruction."

"Haven't you ever heard of the beautiful double or triple rainbows after a good rain?" Joey argued.

"Break's over. If I have any chance of getting my degree, it is back to editing for me and you need to stick that beautiful nose back in your thick textbook."

Joey smiled, retrieved her book from the floor, and returned to her reading.

†

"Must be nice to have a boss who lets you blow off work and clients any time you want," Carolyn grumbled as she leaned against the door-frame of the bedroom.

Sabrina was pulling out clothes and inspecting them before tossing what she deemed acceptable clothing into the suitcase. Joey had mentioned that she should pack layers because you never knew what the weather would be like. She'd also said to bring something nice to wear because she wanted to check out the lodge not too far from Forks. The lodge was supposed to have excellent food featuring local organic offerings.

"What?" she asked absently.

"Never mind. So, is this some sort of romantic weekend?" The scowl on Carolyn's face told the story.

Sabrina stopped packing and walked to Carolyn. "I already told you. Joey and I are just good friends. Without the benefits," she quickly added.

"You should remind her of that because I think she lost the memo."

"Doubtful. Hey, you're going to be okay on your own, right? I know you have the early shift tomorrow, but maybe you and Maribel can hang out or something."

"I'll be fine. Yeah, that's the plan. She's taking me to the club."

Sabrina felt a twinge of fear. "Are you sure that's a good idea? There are a lot of drugs and free-flowing alcohol at the clubs."

"Maribel will be there with me. I doubt she'd let me get sucked into that again. She had a front-row seat to my withdrawal and I believe she cares enough about me to not put me into a situation I can't handle. She has faith in my ability to say no. Besides, alcohol is everywhere, the sooner I decide to be around it and not slide back down Kilimanjaro—ass first—the better. At least one person believes in me."

Sabrina pulled Carolyn into a hug. "I believe in you, hon, I just worry. It's something people do when they care about someone."

Carolyn stepped back from the embrace. "Nice save. You better get back to packing. Joey seems like the type to be on time and I know she wanted to leave the apartment no later than twelve thirty. Frankly, I don't blame her. Seattle traffic sucks. That's the only thing I hate about this city."

Sabrina returned to select clothes for her weekend and was holding out two dresses for consideration. "Which one? The blue or the black?"

"The blue, definitely. It brings out your eyes and screams sexy and classy, versus slutty and common." She pointed to the blue dress on the left. "Although, you look rather scrumptious in the black dress. Why do you care so much? It's not like you're going on a date. On second thought, wear that boring tan one, that screams friend."

"I know, I should toss that horrible thing out. I only bought it because it was on sale for one tenth the original cost. I thought it was the only designer dress I'd ever own. They probably slashed the price so much because it was butt ugly."

Carolyn laughed. "I remember when you brought it home. You were so excited to model it for me, and it took everything in my bag of charm tricks to compliment you on something that was so hideous."

"I remember. You said my ass looked good in the dress. I could tell you hated it. You get that pinched look on your face when you don't like something. You had that look earlier. Are you sure you'll be okay on your own?"

"Stop already. I don't want to feel like a two-year-old around you. No more eggshells. Please?" Carolyn batted her eyes.

"Fine, but we will talk about what set off crinkle face when I get back. Right now, I need to hurry." Sabrina tossed a few casual jerseys and shirts inside the bag, zipped it shut and then carefully laid the dress on top. She thought it was perfect timing when she heard the knock on the door. She was ready. She couldn't contain her excitement, although a part of her dreaded the conversation she knew she would have to have upon her return. She knew Carolyn almost better than anyone and that pinched look on her face wasn't a mystery at all. Carolyn was jealous. She still harbored hope that eventually they would get back together—after a reasonable time during which she proved herself.

Carolyn's gaze seemed to change as she continued to watch Sabrina get ready. An almost serene look of acceptance replaced her pinched expression. "Sabrina, we don't have to talk. It's okay. I want you to be happy. Stop worrying about me, okay? It's all going to work out. Sometimes it's good to let go of the things that hold us back. It's time we both did that." Carolyn kissed Sabrina on the cheek and smiled. Before opening the door to Joey, Sabrina noted with an air of surprise that Carolyn's smile reached her eyes. A genuine smile from Carolyn was a rare occurrence these days.

CHAPTER FOURTEEN

Joey rounded the corner and Lake Crescent in all its glory came into view. The sun had blessed their trip by forming small twinkles on the lake. The rich greenery created a natural picture frame. All the beauty surrounding them finally elicited a verbal response from Sabrina.

"Wow. Okay, that's spectacular. We're about thirty minutes away now, right?"

"Uh huh."

"Can we come back here tomorrow? I'd love to check out the lake and see if there are any walking paths."

"You don't want to see the rainforest tomorrow?" Joey asked.

"Oh, damn. I want to do both. Maybe we should stop and at least take in the view."

165

Joey pulled into a small lookout point and, the minute the car was in park, Sabrina jumped out. She looked at Joey who was now standing next to her. Their bodies were in such close proximity they were almost touching one another. Joey heard the contented sigh escape from Sabrina's mouth and took her hand as she gazed out on the lake. "Thanks for coming with me. I want to talk to you about something, but later, okay?"

"Sure. Hey, do you think Carolyn will be okay on her own?"

Joey released Sabrina's hand and turned away. "Yeah, Maribel will keep her company."

"That's what I'm worried about?"

"Why, are you jealous?"

"No. I just don't think she happens to be the best influence on Carolyn. She hasn't gotten the party girl out of her system yet and that could be dangerous to an addict."

"Maribel cares for Carolyn. And not as a casual one-nighter, either. Now, I'm not saying she's ready for a full-on committed relationship, but I think Maribel has evolved to a kind of dating stage."

"Oh."

"You don't seem thrilled about that piece of information."

"I'm not unhappy. Carolyn's an adult. She can do whatever she wishes, but part of her addiction happens to include sex and Maribel would be the kind of drug that would be hard to resist."

Joey raised her eyebrow. "Hmm. I guess I have two people to compete with now." She winked to mask her uneasiness.

"Stop flirting or I'll take you seriously." Sabrina bumped shoulders with Joey.

"Come on, let's head to the hotel. I want to check out the two choices for dinner."

"Two? You must be joking."

"Nope, the locals said there were only two decent places to eat. I believe I use the word decent generously. I suppose acceptable would be more accurate," Joey explained.

Sabrina groaned. "So that's what I'll be able to look forward to when I visit you during your three-year prison sentence."

Joey turned and lost her jovial expression. "Honestly, I don't enjoy living in Seattle. If I'm completely truthful, I am looking forward to moving to Forks, or at least somewhere a lot less hectic. Small towns suit me. I feel like I can do a lot more good in a place like Forks."

Sabrina tilted her head. "You are full of surprises, Joey Hartford."

"More than you'll ever know." She almost added, unless I continue with my plan to spill out my feelings, raw and unfiltered.

"Ah, that lower pane on Johari's window is alive and well in you. Perhaps you should bring the size of that pane in line with the others."

"I will as soon as you do," Joey quipped back.

†

The accommodations presented an awkward dilemma to Joey and Sabrina. On the edge of town at the Olympic Suites Inn, the hospital had arranged for a suite with only a king-sized bed. Although the Inn was right off of Highway 101, it felt a lot like they had entered a nature retreat. The long driveway curved around into a string of two-story buildings surrounded by an abundance of trees. Besides the blacktop from the driveway and the buildings, no other evidence of civilization was apparent. After Joey strolled back to the car with the key in her hand, Sabrina laughed.

"An actual key, not a key card. Not that I stay in hotels very often, but I haven't seen one of those in years. What have we gotten ourselves into? I sure hope this isn't another Bates motel."

Joey had thought the same thing when the clerk had handed her a key versus the more contemporary keycards that most hotels used. Forks was old school and although they had probably upgraded the rooms from their original seventies' decor, the lock mechanisms remained.

"Quaint, huh?"

"Sure, let's go with that."

Climbing the weathered gray stairs, Joey jiggled the key in the lock until the door opened. Pleasantly surprised by the inside, Joey was about to remark on not judging a book by its cover when she spied the single king-sized bed in the suite.

"I swear, I did not ask for only one bed."

Sabrina laughed. "I didn't think you did."

Joey pointed to the couch in the main living area. "I'll sleep there. Maybe if I'm lucky, it's a pullout."

"Don't be ridiculous. That bed is huge. I'm sure it's large enough for both of us to sleep comfortably. I'm positive I can control myself. Can you?" Sabrina teased.

Joey wasn't convinced that comfort was the right word to use. She would be anything but comfortable with Sabrina by her side all night. She wasn't ready to have the planned conversation before they retired for bed. She could do this. "Course I can. I'm not some sex-crazed heathen."

"Okay, this is nice. There's even a kitchen. We could cook a meal here if we wanted. Is there a grocery store in this little town?"

"I'm sure there is. There would have to be one, right?" Joey hesitantly asked.

Sabrina shrugged. "I guess we'll have to check things out."

"I heard most everything is on the main road. Let's dump our stuff and go exploring. We can plan our evening after seeing what's available. Either we can check out the two fine eateries or find the grocery store. I don't cook, though, so we would have to find something already prepared or easy to fix."

"I'm not the best cook either, but I can make a few simple dishes. Maybe there's fresh fish. We are close to the ocean, you know."

"Fresh fish sounds good."

†

Signs of the *Twilight* craze were everywhere. As they passed what Joey suspected was the main part of town, she liked what she saw. There was an attractive modern-looking building on the left. The curved structure with layers of wood shingles stood out among the other older buildings that adorned the main drag. It was an attractive structure, appearing out-of-place in a town that seemed a bit economically depressed. Joey squinted at the sign that read Rainforest Art Center. She wanted to check the place out, but wasn't sure of the hours and they had so many other places to go. *Maybe another trip,* she thought.

Pacific Pizza was one of the places someone had suggested and although they had come across a grocery store, Joey thought going for some pizza might be easier than trying to prepare something in the suite. The Thriftway was less than two miles down the road and Joey felt the need to pull into the parking lot. She marveled at the Forks Outfitters sign on top of the store adjoined to the Thriftway. She hadn't seen anything like this in many years. She imagined this was like those old-time stores back in the 1800s where the owners stocked every imaginable item a person might need in their local mercantile. Joey thought Mercantile would be a better name for the store in front of her than Outfitters.

"Come on, we have to see what's in that store," Joey declared excitedly.

As Sabrina and Joey strolled through both buildings, Joey noted, "God, this is so awesome. They have everything. It's like a friendly version of Walmart."

"Only without the Walmart prices. Things are kinda expensive here," Sabrina noted.

"I'll be on a doctor's salary; I think I can afford it. Besides, I'd rather give locals the business than drive to the Walmart in Port Angeles, even if the prices are ridiculously better."

"Okay, that seems fair. Supporting the local economy is noble. Are we going to buy dinner here or check out one of the restaurants?"

"I say we check out Pacific Pizza. I'd rather spend my time exploring than cooking. I was teasing when I said it was only decent food. I've been assured it's superb."

"Okay, I'm easy."

Joey grinned. "You are? My, my, have you reverted to the wild and crazy days of your youth?"

Sabrina smacked Joey's chest. "You know what I meant."

Joey laughed. "A gal can dream, you know."

†

Sabrina had to admit she enjoyed the whole communing with nature thing after she had explored the rain forest with Joey. The tangled roots covered in moss depicted a kind of beauty she hadn't ever experienced. Her favorite place was a thick-trunked tree curving over top of the path, creating a natural arch. Moss covered the trunk like tinsel on a Christmas tree. She hadn't minded the light mist that fell on and off throughout the day. Packing her rain jacket had been a smart move.

Joey had joked that Forks was famous for the abrupt weather changes. When the clouds had finally disappeared, and the sun made its glorious move, Sabrina appreciated spending the time at the beach. She could hardly believe she was at the Pacific Ocean. Kalaloch Lodge sat on top of the cliffs. The surrounding landscape wasn't anything like any version of the ocean she had expected. Lush vegetation sprouting out of the cliffs replaced visions of warm water and California beaches. The gnarled trunks on the trees reminded Sabrina of an old woman with arthritis and that made her sad until she looked at Joey taking everything in. There was such an innocent joy on her face that Sabrina had to look beyond the image of pain that traveled through her mind when she thought of that old woman. She pushed her grandmother's hands out of her mind and focused on the view. It had always been uncomfortable to watch how debilitating that autoimmune disease was and now her mother was showing signs in her own joints.

Driftwood was everywhere. The remaining wisps of clouds helped to create a different sunset over the ocean. She wanted to mark this memory and pulled out her cell phone to take a picture.

Joey took her hand again like she'd done yesterday and led her to a large piece of driftwood. She didn't let go when they sat.

"So, how was dinner? Not bad for a place in the middle of nowhere. It's an easy jaunt from Forks. I suspect this might become a favorite hangout for me, despite the forty-minute drive."

"I shouldn't say this because it sounds so rude, but yes, it was surprisingly good. The pizza yesterday also exceeded my expectations. This has been such a wonderful day and evening. Again, thank you for inviting me. Now, are you going to tell me what's got you so nervous?"

"Maybe." Joey grinned.

Sitting so close to Joey, Sabrina felt the buzz of Joey's phone and looked down at her jacket pocket where Joey had hidden it away.

"Your pocket is buzzing."

"I should ignore it."

"It's probably one of your hook ups seeing if you have a free hour or two."

Joey frowned. "I spend all my free time with you. I don't do the hook up thing anymore."

"You don't?"

Joey shoved against Sabrina with her shoulder. "No, I don't and I'm hurt you haven't noticed."

"Sorry. You should check your phone to see who called now that—" Sabrina was about to finish her sentence when the buzzing began again. "Answer it because someone is desperately trying to get ahold of you."

"Hello," Joey answered. "Whoa, whoa, slow down, Maribel. Hang on. Is it okay if I put you on speaker? Sabrina is right here." Joey pressed the button and Maribel's panicked voice rang through the speaker.

"It was just a little weed, but she started kinda freaking out. Talking about a pie with a bunch of little scenes like in a movie or something. Then she said they were spinning around and she grabbed her head and started rocking."

"Fucking hell, Maribel. Why did you give her marijuana?" Joey yelled.

"She was kinda down. I think she misses Sabrina. I wanted to help her relax a little. It's not like I gave her some illegal drug. She was all stressed out about being an ass with Sabrina. Honest, I was trying to be a good friend. You know, listen and maybe offer something to have her wind down a little. I promise, I didn't make a move on her. How was I to know Derick gave me the stuff laced with something a little extra? What should I do?"

"Take her home and get her tucked into bed while whatever the pot was laced with works itself out. Don't leave her alone either," Joey directed.

"We'll be back in four hours. Please don't let anything bad happen to her. If things get worse, call." Sabrina barely managed to control the shake in her voice.

†

Joey was making small circles in Sabrina's back. "I'll take you back if that's what you want to do, but..."

"What? Go ahead, you've never held back before."

"Look, if we go back tonight, I think it might be a signal to her. A message I hope you aren't intending to give."

"What do you mean 'it might be a signal'?"

"Figure out what you want, Sabrina. Either way, going back tonight won't be the right answer. It might seem like it to Carolyn because she'll convince herself it's because you're choosing her. But the secondary message is that you don't trust her enough for her to stand on her own."

"I'm not choosing anyone. Being a good friend to someone means being there for them no matter what. I trust her, I don't trust Maribel."

"She will probably stumble here and there and that's okay to do. Every single one of us stumbles and makes bad decisions from time to time. That isn't reserved for addicts. It isn't the end of the world, Sabrina. She didn't choose the hard stuff. I'm not so sure it's a bad thing to test the boundaries of clean and sober. Maybe that's not a popular view. This might be as much a test for you as it is for her. If you treat this as a major relapse, so will she. Her version of who she is will be reflected in your eyes. Your opinion and approval matters to her. Not going back says you have enough faith in her ability to evaluate what happened and make a better decision the next time around. You were there for her when she needed you."

"God, I hate it when you're so right and I'm the one who should be spitting out this good advice."

"Yeah, that's me all right. A good friend whose only purpose is to offer stupendous counsel when prompted. Certainly not anyone's choice," Joey grumbled.

Sabrina turned Joey's face with her hand. "Hey, talk to me. What's going on in that beautiful head of yours? I think that's the first time I've ever detected a hard edge to your voice."

"Honestly. Are you sure you want the unbridled version of what I'm thinking right now?"

"Well, yeah, always."

"Actions speak louder than words." Joey pulled Sabrina close and placed her lips gently at first and then when there wasn't any resistance, she deepened the kiss by sucking Sabrina's bottom lip and then pushing her tongue inside almost tentatively. When Joey heard Sabrina moan, she wanted to stay entwined in the embrace and continue the kiss, but finally let it come to its natural conclusion and broke free while continuing to hold her.

"I want you and not just as a friend. And I'm terrified you don't feel the same way or you're waiting for Carolyn to get a little healthier before telling her you're willing to try again. Or even worse, you haven't figured out what you want, and I won't have closure one way or another. So many terrible things are running through my head right now. I'm sorry."

Sabrina had a stunned expression on her face. "Okay, that was so not what I was expecting."

"That's all you have to say? Shit, Sabrina, either put me out of my misery and tell me I don't have a chance or..."

"Um, you have to give me a few moments to process this dramatic course correction."

"I guess that's my answer." Joey pushed away and walked quickly down the beach.

Sabrina ran to catch up. "Joey, wait. I'm anything but impulsive. Am I attracted to you? Definitely. Have I thought about more than a friendship with you? That would be another yes. But..."

"I hate that word 'but,' it always means I'm not getting what I want and someone is going to patiently explain to me why not."

"You were the one who established the boundaries..."

"Women change their minds all the time. Please, can we stay and we'll visit my author friend tomorrow. Maybe after I corrupt you enough to get you to steal a pair of panties, I can convince you to..."

"Ruin your last year of medical school?"

"Don't be dramatic. You won't be ruining anything. In ten years, I'm sure it isn't going to matter one lick if I graduate at the top of my class, but it will matter if you aren't in my life anymore. I think my priorities were all out of whack. Time for a reshuffling, don't you think? Unless you haven't figured stuff out yet. I hate falling for processors." Joey grabbed Sabrina's hand and pulled her to her feet. "Come on, we can decide on the way back to Forks if we're driving another four hours tonight or not. At least I will have forty minutes to talk sense in you."

†

By the time they returned to the Inn, Sabrina was feeling a little more settled. Joey was right, it wasn't like Carolyn had scored heroin. She hadn't completely explored her feelings about marijuana use yet. For someone who didn't have a problem with drugs, she didn't have an issue. However, for addicts, she hadn't arrived at a definitive conclusion yet. She knew about the promising results related to CBD use, the chemical property derived from marijuana.

"What do you think was laced with the marijuana Maribel gave to Carolyn?" Sabrina asked as Joey opened the door to the suite.

"I don't know, maybe it wasn't laced at all. There are some strong varieties these days that can sometimes cause a negative reaction. From what Maribel described, I know it sounds bad, but I believe taking her to a quiet place will resolve things. In four hours, I doubt there will be any residual effects."

"So you're saying that heading back now won't help one bit."

Joey shrugged. "The only person it might help is you, if it gives you a small peace of mind. I'm happy to drive us back if that's what it will take to remove that panicked look on your face."

"You're exaggerating. I can't possibly have that crazed look because I am feeling more comfortable about waiting until tomorrow to head back."

"Maybe that panicked look is more about sharing a bed with me after my lack of impulse control," Joey answered.

Sabrina shook her head. "No, if there is one thing I'm sure of, it's that you would never do anything to push me into something I'm not ready for. Don't even think about suggesting you sleep on an uncomfortable pull-out bed."

"Mind reader."

"Psht, those nonverbals of yours are screaming at me."

"So...breakfast at my friend's house and then back to civilization?" Joey asked.

"Yup that's the plan. And thanks, Joey. I needed someone to talk sense into me. I should not make a bigger deal of this than it is." Sabrina laughed. "I remember when my mom showed me that movie, *Reefer Madness*. They used to scare kids with that. I don't really believe pot is a gateway drug. My mother thought it was absolutely hysterical and I have to admit I doubled over laughing when she shared it with me."

"I have to meet this mother of yours."

"I hope you do someday. You two would get along," Sabrina answered.

CHAPTER FIFTEEN

"Breakfast. We'll leave after breakfast. And if you must, go ahead and call Maribel to see how Carolyn is doing. 'Cause I know you're going to ignore what she told us last night. I'm sure it was that call after we returned to the hotel that cemented your decision, and not my wise words that got you to stay. My author friend is dying to meet you and she says her French toast is to die for. I'm making an exception to eat that less than healthy breakfast, just for you."

"We could take our time heading back, huh? We did say we'd be back tonight." Although the conversation wasn't exactly stilted, Sabrina recognized Joey's reluctance to push Sabrina regarding the nature of their friendship and the possibility of more. That was fine and dandy with her because she still wasn't sure where she landed on the whole idea. The kiss had been nice. Better than nice. It had been electrifying if she were honest with herself. She almost blurted out, "We should talk about the kiss and everything else," but she played along. Today's agenda was prance around the elephant in the room. As she processed the events of the previous evening, she had to admit she was not unaffected by sleeping next to Joey all night long, despite the size of the bed.

"Yes, we did." Joey smiled. "Besides, I was hoping to take you on the short trail by Crescent Lake."

"I wanted to do that. What time are we supposed to arrive for this gourmet breakfast?"

"Around nineish." Joey turned over her wrist and glanced at her watch. "It's a quarter 'til right now, but I wouldn't worry too much. There isn't anywhere in Forks you can't get to within five minutes. Her place is up the road a mile or two. Don't forget to fawn over her babies."

"I thought you said she was old enough to be your mother."

"She is. Her fur babies. I think she's up to seven."

"Oh my God, I am totally stereotyping now. I can see how recluse writer and crazy cat-lady go together. Like peanut butter and jelly."

"She's not really a recluse, but she lives like seven hours away from her wife and I think that's taken a toll on her. I saw a slight change in her writing style this past year. Maybe it's because of the long-distance thing or maybe it's the Trump effect. Hard to say." Joey shrugged. "She's still a little quirky and a lot of fun."

Joey draped her arm over Sabrina's shoulder and led her from the room. They drove the short distance to the office that bordered the large cluster of trees. There was clearly not a shortage of trees in Forks. Joey jumped out and dropped off the key.

✝

By the time they reached the modest home, the slight awkwardness subsided to make room for their easy exchange. Sabrina liked the look of the house surrounded by more trees covered in droplets of water after the rain showers of the previous evening.

"So, you need to follow my lead if you're going to come away from this morning adventure with your very own pair of stolen panties." Joey winked.

"I am so not stealing a pair of underwear."

"Oh yes, you are. I want something to lord over you and up to now you've given me zip. Besides, I sort of explained my whole stealth plan to my friend, and she's totally down with the idea. She expects it." Joey undid her seat belt and exited the car.

Hanging back, Joey waited for Sabrina and they walked up the driveway to the front door.

"Well, then I plan to buy a book or two of hers. You said she was giving them out with her books that'll make me feel like less of a criminal."

"Fine, Miss Goody Two Shoes." Joey knocked on the shiny wood door that looked like it had recently received a coating of shellac.

"That is such an old-fashioned saying—Miss Goody Two Shoes. What, were you born in the fifties?"

"Meanie. I'll bet you were one of those mean girls in high school."

"I most certainly was not."

181

"Yeah, me neither. I was a studious jock. You better toss out that horrible notion you have in your brain that intelligent jocks don't exist. The two are not mutually exclusive."

"I was not going to say that at all. I think someone is projecting."

The heavy wood door opened and creaked a little as a petite woman appeared in the doorway and opened her arms.

"Joey. Damn, if only I wasn't married and three times your age."

"Annabelle, practicing your writing embellishment I see. Three times my age, seriously?" Joey embraced the older woman and then took a step back and gestured to Sabrina. "This is my friend, Sabrina. Be careful what you say to her, though, she might psychoanalyze you and frankly she'd have a lot to work with."

Annabelle laughed. "Great to meet you." She held out her hand. "Oh, and by the way, I'm calling my exaggerations hyperbole now. I like how that word rolls off my tongue. Besides, if it's good enough for our shitty president, it should apply to fiction writers as well."

"Ugh, can we please not talk about him? I've been eagerly waiting for your famed French toast and I don't want to lose my appetite."

"Come in, come in. Hurry up before one of my cats makes a run for it. Most of them are hiding, but I'm sure Yazdi will make an appearance. She's the friendly one."

Almost on cue, a multi-colored longhaired cat wove in and out of their legs.

Sabrina leaned down to pet her and cooed, "Oh aren't you a pretty little girl." Sabrina felt the rumble at the same time she heard the loud purr.

"She's my little cuddle bunny. Likes to sleep by my side and keep me company. Thank God, because I desperately miss my wife and Yazdi's the only thing keeping me sane."

"Joey told me. That's rough. Hopefully, your writing keeps you occupied."

"It does," Annabelle answered.

"Hey, after breakfast, can you bring out the famed suitcase full of books and panties? I think Sabrina wants to purchase at least one signed copy of one of your books." Joey winked at Annabelle as she followed her inside the modest house.

Three place settings surrounded a vase of simple flowers. Sabrina wasn't an expert on plants. Other than identifying roses or daises, she wasn't sure what the colorful array of pinks, reds, yellows, and oranges were as they sat in the middle of the table.

"Coffee?" Annabelle asked.

"Oh God, yes," Joey answered and Sabrina nodded.

Annabelle pointed to the beautiful table. "Sit, I'll grab the French toast from the oven and get your coffee. Cream and sugar are on the table. I know you two are on a tight schedule today, so I'm thrilled you stopped by."

"So, how's the new book coming?" Joey asked.

"Meh. You know I'm doing another collaboration. It started as a joke. Which if I'm honest, half of my books or stories start that way. Anyway, you know how I hate to write sex scenes. Since this book is about lesbian sex workers, it's almost mandatory for me to include steamy sex scenes. Ugh. I'm struggling. Good thing my partner in crime is good at it and can give me some pointers." Annabelle set two steaming cups of coffee in front of Sabrina and Joey, then turned back toward the kitchen to pull the stack of toast from the oven.

Joey laughed. "You do fine and I've seen tremendous growth in that area."

"I should have the draft to you in another month or so." After she set the plate of food on top of the hotplate next to the vase, she pointed to it and said, "Dig in while it's still hot."

Joey wasn't shy about helping herself to three large pieces of toast. Sabrina started with one and was happy to see both syrup and various jams on the table.

Sabrina picked up the knife setting next to her plate and stuck it in the strawberry jam scooping out a generous amount to add to her one piece of toast. "I didn't know there were other folks who eat French toast with anything but syrup."

Annabelle waved her hand in the air. "Oh, I don't, but Joey said you did, so I pulled out the homemade jams I picked up at the farmer's market."

Sabrina glanced at Joey with an appraising look. She could only remember once that she'd ordered French toast and marveled at how Joey must have recalled that detail. "Well, aren't you a basket of surprises, Joey Hartford?"

"That's what makes her such a wonderful beta. She pays attention to details."

"If I can be so bold to ask, why panties as a giveaway?" Sabrina inquired.

"That was another joke that took on a life of its own. A reader posted about their aversion to the word panties. I had to do a whole panties week thing to desensitize readers and then thought instead of T-shirts it might be fun to slap covers onto different styles of panties. I got a little crazy and kept buying more panties. The rest, they say, is history. I had fun with it."

"I'll admit to being fascinated with the boi shorts with the fun designs ironed on them. I saw Joey's and since I am still looking for the perfect fitting panty, I was tempted to steal one."

"Aren't we all," Annabelle responded.

"Aren't we all what?" Sabrina asked.

"Looking for the perfect fitting underwear." Annabelle laughed. "Joey told me about your fascination with her undergarments. The boi shorts are very comfy. I put on one of the pairs I made and I think I'm in love. I haven't modeled them for my wife yet. I like the way they feel, but not the way they look. My muffin top is overly exaggerated in the boi shorts, so I am not sure I like that. Do you have time for one last cup of coffee and then I can bring out the famed suitcase? I have to warn you, I am an acquired taste. I'm a bit quirky, but I do have a wide variety of books to choose from." She grinned.

As Joey and Sabrina made themselves comfortable on Annabelle's overstuffed cream-colored couch, the author exited the room and returned with a rolling suitcase.

"Wow, is that luggage full of books and underwear?" Sabrina asked.

Annabelle nodded, then unzipped the case and showed her wares. "Go ahead, paw through the unmentionables to check them out and the books."

Sabrina grabbed a book with what looked like a painting of a woman on the cover. The bright colors and sort of abstract quality about the cover caught her attention. She turned the book over and read the description. "This looks interesting."

"Oh, it is," Joey answered. "One of my favorites because it was so different. I think you'll like it. The main character is bi-polar and is represented quite positively. A heroine."

"Okay, sold."

"You should also get this one." Joey picked up the one with the woman who appeared to be enjoying the fall leaves. "In my humble opinion this book is her best work to date."

Sabrina took the book from Joey's hand and once again turned it over to read the back. "Interesting. Okay, I'll get them both. How much? Will you sign them for me?"

"Of course. How about twenty dollars? And with a two-book purchase—"

"Don't you need to get a pen?" Joey interrupted.

Annabelle's face scrunched up in confusion and then, as if a lightbulb had gone off, a broad smile blossomed on her face. "Oh yes, right. I need my special pen."

After she left, Joey twitched her eyes toward the suitcase and jerked her head in a silent gesture for Sabrina to do something. Sabrina wasn't sure what she was trying to tell her until Joey whispered, "Go ahead, now's your chance."

"I'm not taking a pair of panties."

"Hurry before she comes back."

An insane rush came over Sabrina and she grabbed a pair of boi shorts sitting on top. They were the color of a demon or devil—red. And she thought that was apropos for what she was about to do. She stuffed them down her bra and grinned.

"Nice," Joey responded. "Good choice, by the way." Joey laughed uncontrollably as Annabelle returned.

"It sounds like I missed something good. Sabrina, your face is bright red right now."

"Um, no, Joey is just being Joey," she explained before pulling a twenty from her purse and handing it to Annabelle.

Annabelle uncapped her pen and scribbled something on the first page. The two women made the exchange between books and money.

Joey stood and announced, "We better get going if we have any chance of exploring the lake before heading back to Seattle. Thanks, Annabelle. Happy writing."

Annabelle walked them to the door and they both made a quick beeline to Joey's car. As soon as they shut the doors, Joey and Sabrina broke into a fit of giggles.

"Well done, Sabrina. Your first pair of stolen panties."

"I can't believe you set this up ahead of time."

"Everyone has to start somewhere." Joey grinned.

CHAPTER SIXTEEN

As Joey pulled into the parking lot of the lodge, she turned to Sabrina and asked, "Are you sure you want to check out this trail? I heard the falls are a must-see around these parts and it's only a short trek, but we can head back and skip this little side trip."

"Nah. I checked this trail out and it shouldn't take long. I'm not sure when I'll have the chance again to visit this beautiful place. Let's do it."

"Well, I'm not sure I like that answer. Does that mean you categorically refuse to visit me?"

Sabrina scrubbed her face with her hand. "God, no. I might consider working at that little behavioral health clinic. I got a good feel and it would be tempting to go somewhere I can make a difference. We'll see."

188

With that last statement Joey jumped from the vehicle and ran to Sabrina's side to take her hand. A tiny spark of hope grew inside as their hands intertwined. The weather wasn't as nice as the other evening at the beach and Sabrina let go to pull up her hood. The tiny droplets of rain dripped to the ground with a few making their way to her eyelashes before she sought cover under her hood. Joey felt a true sense of loss when Sabrina stuck her hands in her pockets, but understood her attempt to keep away the slight chill.

They walked along the path in relative silence. Joey was biting her tongue to keep from bringing forward the topic she'd broached after the call from Maribel. Space. Sabrina needed space right now.

Sabrina turned her head and gave Joey a side glance. "I promise, we'll talk about things, but not right now. Today I want to enjoy this time with you and commune with nature. I need that little breather."

The leaves on the rickety bridge along with the crude wood stairs created more of a hazard than Joey felt comfortable with. As she held out her hand to help provide stability, Sabrina accepted the offering and removed her hand from the warm pocket in her jacket.

"Watch your steps, the wet leaves and mud make this a little tricky to navigate."

"It's so beautiful with all the hanging moss and the different shades of green. This was totally worth it. Although I think the climb is a subtle message I need to work out more." Sabrina's labored breathing increased. "God this is embarrassing. You're not even breaking a sweat or breathing heavy at all."

"You want me breathing heavy, huh? Well, all you gotta do is—"

"Do not finish that thought, Joey Hartford. You are such an incessant flirt."

"I like how you say my first and last name." Joey's voice was soft and filled with emotion.

They reached the top of the trail and Sabrina leaned against the uneven wood rail. She once again broke contact with Joey to remove the cell phone from her jacket pocket and took pictures of the falls. Joey tested the wood by pushing against the railing, making sure it was stable enough.

The water seemed to start as a narrow stream and then feathered outward in a series of streams looking a bit like a whitewater broom until it reached the placid pool. The falls weren't massive but, nestled among the rocks and foliage, this was a sight more beautiful than Niagara Falls in Joey's humble opinion. The air had that fresh earthy smell—rain, leaves, and dirt mingled together. Joey breathed in deeply to allow the odor a chance to penetrate her senses.

"I'm not very adept at selfies, but I want one with you."

Joey held out her hand. "Gimme. I have long arms; I'll take the picture. Then are you ready to head back?"

"Yeah, I am. Do you want me to drive? You've been doing all the driving so far and that can't be very relaxing."

"I don't mind driving at all. If I'm honest, I'm a control freak when it comes to driving. I don't make a very good passenger. Fortunately, I don't have to endure that too often in Seattle. I wouldn't make a good patient either." Joey walked down the path with the old uneven planks wedged into the ground and offered her hand to Sabrina again who readily took it.

"Good to know. I will have to tuck that away for future use. Does that need for control happen to extend to other parts of your life?" Sabrina abruptly stopped on a large flat area between the next set of stairs. "Never mind. Don't answer that question. Just strike that from the record."

Joey laughed. "Ah, what has been heard cannot be unheard. And no, I'd like to think I am a bit egalitarian in the bedroom. Top. Bottom. I go with the flow."

"So...new topic. Shall I strangle Maribel with my bare hands when we get back or use another form of punishment for her bone-headed move last night?"

"Um, I wouldn't talk about it as a form of punishment. You might get a wholly different reaction from what you intend. I'd go with a punch to the throat. I don't believe that has ever been considered a form of foreplay."

Sabrina raised her eyebrow. "Are you into that?"

"No, no, not me. Seriously, though, I might go easy on Maribel. She doesn't always make the best decisions, but none of us do all the time. I don't believe she had nefarious motivations for offering Carolyn a little dope. Nor do I think she thought it would be a big deal. She likes Carolyn." Joey waggled her eyebrows. "You know she 'likes-her likes her' as in the *check box yes* on a passed school note back in my mother's day. My mom used to make me watch reruns of *The Wonder Years* and doubled over in laughter every time she heard that line. She said the show got everything correct. Then she proceeded to tell me she got her first note from a boy when she was nine, asking, *do you like me* with little boxes next to yes and no for answers."

"That's adorable."

"Mom would have been sixty this year had she lived." Joey felt a twinge of sadness at the memory.

"I'm sorry." Sabrina moved closer to Joey. "Mine came in a text message."

"From a girl or a boy?"

"Both."

"So are you saying you might have been pansexual at an early age before you entered that sex shop?"

"Nope, I dashed the poor boy's hopes and answered yes to the girl. I haven't looked back since."

"Liar," Joey declared.

Sabrina crossed her chest. "Nope, I swear it's all true. I was ahead of my time at the ripe old age of eleven. I never understood the angst. I knew and acted like it was the most normal thing in the world to like girls *that way* instead of boys."

"Good on you."

"Weren't you the same?" Sabrina asked.

"Let's just say, I was a late bloomer. If you can call blooming in your senior year of high school late."

"But look at how nicely you bloomed." Sabrina winked.

"Careful, I might kiss you again after that flirtatious comment."

Sabrina pulled on Joey's arm and then let go and began running down the path. "Last one to the car is a rotten fishhead."

Joey laughed and chased after Sabrina. "Fishhead? How utterly Northwest of you."

†

Sabrina had leaned back against the seat of Joey's borrowed car, and before she knew it, she'd fallen asleep. The motion of a car always seemed to lull her to a relaxed state. When they hit Seattle and the start-and-stop traffic materialized, she woke and made her apologies for being such a terrible passenger. Joey waved her apology away.

She invited Joey to come inside, not trusting her ability to keep her irritation with Maribel in check. Joey would be a great buffer. After dumping the bags on the floor, Sabrina heard the quiet moans coming from her bedroom. Thinking Maribel had left Carolyn on her own and she was in distress, she rushed into the bedroom. Joey tried to stop her by attempting to grab her arm, but she was too quick.

"What the hell," Sabrina called out.

"Shit, shit, shit. I thought you were coming home later tonight." Carolyn grabbed for the sheet to cover up, but not before Joey and Sabrina caught the full naked view of both women. Maribel turned over, looking wide-eyed at Joey and Sabrina.

Sabrina pivoted on her heels and shut the bedroom door behind her. Joey opened her mouth, but closed it after Sabrina shook her head. "Your apartment and wine. Lots of wine."

"You don't want to check on Carolyn?"

"Nope, I don't. I think Maribel is thoroughly checking her out from the brief view I got."

"Okay," Joey hesitantly responded.

In the background Sabrina could hear a faint rustling of activity and low rumbling voices. As Joey and Sabrina reached the door, she heard a bang as her bedroom door flung open.

"Sabrina wait," Carolyn called out.

"Nope. I don't want or need an explanation. You're an adult. We aren't together. End of story," Sabrina called over her shoulder as she closed the door to her apartment and quickly made her way to Joey's. The last thing she heard before the door closed was, "fuck."

†

The door to Joey's apartment had barely closed before Sabrina grabbed Joey, spun her around, and then pushed her up against the wall. The bruising kiss that followed startled Joey for a few seconds before she gently pushed her away.

"Whoa, whoa, stop, Sabrina."

"Why?" Sabrina's genuinely perplexed expression mixed with sadness was almost Joey's undoing. "I thought you didn't always have to be in control. So...I guess you get to initiate a kiss, but I don't?"

"Not like this. Not when you're angry, frustrated, hurt...shit, Sabrina, I don't know because you won't talk to me while you're still processing." Joey placed a finger on Sabrina's head. "I can't know what's rolling around in that pretty head of yours if you won't let me in."

"Is it too much to ask for once, just once, that I was the center of someone's universe?"

"No, definitely not, but, hon, you have to be willing to return the favor."

"God, how can you always be right? Sometimes I don't like that about you."

Joey pulled Sabrina into an embrace and made small circles on her back. "Fibber. I think that's the one thing I have going for me. The ability to evaluate something from every angle. Without emotion or the rest of that stuff that gets us in trouble. Except, of course, when it comes to me and you. I had visions of the perfect weekend and that didn't work out the way I wanted," she whispered while still holding Sabrina.

Joey let her arms fall to her sides and then grabbed Sabrina's hand. "Come on, let's talk. I'll bring you wine and lots of it if that's what you want, but I suggest we do this completely sober."

Sabrina seemed to lose all of her fire and meekly followed Joey to the couch. "Fine. No wine." Almost dejectedly, Sabrina sat on the couch.

Still holding Sabrina's hand, Joey turned her body to face Sabrina with one leg folded and perched on the sofa between them. "What's got you so upset about seeing Carolyn and Maribel together?"

"Now that is the hundred-thousand-dollar question, isn't it?" Sabrina looked to the ceiling. "It's strange, you know, because deep down, I know that Carolyn and I are not meant to be. I love her, but I'm no longer in love with her if that makes sense."

"Perfectly. So then why the reaction?"

"I guess it felt good to have her still want me. For her to still be in love with me."

"Okay, but what if there's someone else out there for you to love who could easily fall in love with you? Maybe already has and you're hanging on to something that will never be."

"Are you talking about you?"

"Yeah, I am. But I need to leave myself out of this for now. Let's go with someone, anyone that's not Carolyn. If you know it'll never work for you two, but you keep her close in your life, dangling on the very thin thread, a massive wall will separate you from anyone else trying to get through."

"You've managed to punch a hole in the wall. I guess stealing panties is not the only thing you're good at stealing."

"Well, apparently the hole is only big enough for my face to peek through. Try as I might to steal you and pull you over to my side that hole ain't big enough for you or me to fit through."

"What are we going to do about that?"

"I think that's up to you. I believe I've made my position clear. Either you remove a few more bricks, or you might as well patch up the hole and let me go. I can't be your best friend anymore, Sabrina. It's too hard for me." Joey looked away.

A loud bang on the door interrupted the heartfelt confession followed by Carolyn yelling, "Sabrina, please, let me in. Let's talk."

"Go figure it out, and when you're ready to tell me what's up, call me." Joey brushed Sabrina's cheek. "Sabrina, don't hang on to any preconceived ideas about what you think is going on. And don't let history define things for Carolyn, or yourself. Listen, really listen to her and to yourself." She moved her hand to right over Sabrina's heart. "The answer is right here. You promise?"

Sabrina nodded, moved to the door, took a big breath, and then opened it. She grabbed Carolyn's arm and said, "Let's take a walk. I think the fresh air will be good for both of us."

Carolyn made a face. "It's raining outside."

"No, it's drizzling. Don't be a wuss. Water is cleansing."

"You've lived too long in Seattle," Carolyn grumbled.

"You wanna talk, that's my condition."

"Can I at least grab my rain jacket? You have yours." Involuntarily shivering, Carolyn looked pointedly at Sabrina.

"Sure."

CHAPTER SEVENTEEN

The light rain had subsided by the time Carolyn and Sabrina walked onto the sidewalk just outside the apartment building. The cloud cover was still heavy and the light gray above didn't appear to show any break in the clouds. Sabrina believed it was highly likely that the rain would return before they finished talking, but for now she pushed back her hood.

Walking at a leisurely pace, Sabrina broke the silence. "Why do you feel the need to explain anything? You're a grown woman."

"Why do you feel the need to display your disappointment face?"

"I didn't—"

"Oh yes, you most certainly did. Somehow, you have a way of reducing me to a naughty child. I always feel like I'm breaking a very important invisible rule."

"I'm sorry. I don't mean to do that. I know that I'm not always aware of my nonverbal signals. Honestly, I think that's true for most people."

"Probably. So why the reaction?"

"I think it's because, for a while there, I was the center of your universe. I know it's selfish of me, but it was nice knowing you were still in love with me."

"Oh, Sabrina. I do still love you, but I'm not in love with you anymore. That was a merry-go-round I had no intention of climbing back on, considering you are clearly in love with someone else."

"I'm not—"

"You are, but we'll talk about that in a few minutes. Please listen carefully to what I have to say."

Sabrina chuckled. "Joey said the same thing."

"She's a smart woman. You should listen to her. I like her, by the way. You have my blessing."

"I thought we weren't going to go there yet."

"Right, back to you listening. No interruptions. Sabrina, I'm way too vain to settle for a love based on obligation or pity. You were always my rock, the lighthouse I gravitated to when the seas were stormy and I needed a little something to help me find my way. I don't want or need that anymore. I want to fuck up a little here and there. Make mistakes, then learn from them. Judge myself, not have others judge me. I can't do that with you. No offense, but you wouldn't let me grow in ways I need to. You'll smother me with that kind of love. I really like Maribel. You may not believe this, but we weren't just having sex. I like that she's far from perfect and

I don't have to live up to some impossible standard with her."

"Okay. I guess that makes sense. What about commitment? I'm not being mean or anything, but I don't see either one of you making the effort."

"Not right now, no, but that's not a prerequisite for either one of us. We both think it's possible to show we care about the other without tying them down. Maybe in the future we'll get there. Don't give me that pinched look. Not everyone defines successful relationships in exactly the same way."

"I think I'm a dinosaur and unfortunately they're extinct. I'm probably the last woman on earth that's still in her twenties who doesn't do casual anymore. I never want to go back to the way I was. Ever."

"Are you referring to Joey's previous extracurricular activities with Maribel?"

Sabrina nodded.

"I'll bet you didn't know Joey hasn't had sex with any other person since that first day you two met in the laundry room?"

"I don't believe that."

Carolyn quirked her eyebrow. "Seriously? How can you not believe me? When would she have time? She spends every free moment she has with you or helping you out with fuck ups like me. Didn't she take you to Forks to confess her undying love? I would have bet everything I hope to have in the future on that."

"She might have mentioned having feelings for me, but no she didn't quite go as far as telling me she's fallen in love or anything like that."

"Were you listening? Or did you block her out? You do that sometimes when you're not ready to hear something."

"I was listening. Don't be mean."

"I think Joey is perfect for you. She has enough playfulness in her to keep you on your toes, but not so much that you repel one another. While opposites attract, there is a limit to how much two people can be different. Take us for example. I'm the look for a nanosecond long enough to see the cool, blue water below before I leap. And of course, the kind of person to scream with joy all the way down. After you shed that wild skin that didn't fit, you became the type to hire a gaggle of scientists to test the water temperature, measure the height of the cliff, and determine the likely trajectory. Then after all that looking, you'll decide not to leap. You're twenty-six, Sabrina, not sixty-six. Leap already."

"I stole a pair of panties," Sabrina blurted out.

Carolyn wrinkled her brow. "Joey's?"

"No, a perfect stranger. Well, she was a friend of Joey's, but I'd never met her before."

"Get out! You did not."

"I did too."

"Prove it," Carolyn challenged.

"Okay, I will. When we get back to the apartment, I'll show you. They even have a book cover ironed on the butt. I have to admit it was a little exhilarating."

"Well flip me over and slap my ass, Joey did something I never could in the whole time we were together—get you to live a little and lighten up. She's definitely a keeper. Listen, I believe you. You don't have to prove it. In fact, I have a little favor to ask. See, Maribel is still back at the apartment and well... I told her to stay put. Can you crash at Joey's tonight? I prefer to handle these little things like adults instead of the sophomoric sock on the door."

"You're joking?" Sabrina glared.

Carolyn batted her eyes. "Please? I know Joey won't mind."

"You're actually asking if you can continue your sexcapades in my bed."

"Well, it is way more comfortable than the futon. Sabrina, I mean this in the nicest way...fucking leap already. It's about time. Go...jump Joey's fine ass. Oh, and after that, I want all the details on this underwear adventure. You'll have to teach me how to do it without getting caught. I'm already salivating over the idea. It sounds so deliciously naughty."

Sabrina shook her head. "I suppose I could ask Joey if I can crash at her place. That doesn't mean we're going to hook up."

"Ri-i-ight. But you want to, don't you? Come on, admit it. For once in your life, admit to a resurfacing of those deep dark urges you almost seem to control."

"Fine. I might have considered that."

Carolyn grinned and looped her arm through Sabrina's. "Let's head back. Our women are waiting for us."

"Hmm, that almost sounded a bit possessive and a lot like a possible commitment." Sabrina smiled at Carolyn. "I do love you and I hope we can stay friends because I need a few zany, spontaneous, live life to the fullest people in my life, and right now you're it until I forgive Maribel."

"Yeah, and I need a few people in my life with the ability to get me not to act on every single impulse."

†

Joey was restless as she paced her cramped apartment. She'd opted for the studio version because it was the cheapest. She was second-guessing her pseudo ultimatum. Maybe she was too harsh on Sabrina. Clearly she was confused about her feelings and Joey hadn't helped by pushing her.

"Fuckity, fuck, fuck," she muttered.

Time to grovel before the woman and beg for her forgiveness. She was too blunt. Joey would tell Sabrina that she should take all the time she needed and Joey would be right there by her side. Friend, lover, whatever she needed. She'd be there. She reached for the doorknob because she had to get some fresh air and prepare herself for the massive apology she needed to make. Before she reached the door, she heard the light knocking.

Puzzled, she opened the door and couldn't believe that the object of her desire was standing there. Looking sheepish, no less.

"Hey," Sabrina said.

Joey pulled Sabrina inside and crushed her body against her own. The hurried words flew out of her mouth, "I'm sorry, so sorry. I am such an asshole. I'll take whatever you can give me. I need you in my life. If it's as friends and that's all it will ever be, I'll gladly take it." She worried that her apology wouldn't be enough.

"Oey, or'e othering me."

"What?" Joey loosened her hold. She was still holding Sabrina so tightly she didn't understand her response.

"Um, the hug was a little overzealous. I merely pointed out you were smothering me and that is not your style. I'm the incessant smotherer. You made the favor I'm about to ask of you incredibly easy. Can I crash at your place tonight?"

"Huh? Back that I'm-totally-flummoxed train up. Of course you can stay here, but why would you want to do that after I was a total jerkwad?"

"Short version, Carolyn and Maribel want some alone time and I'm jumping into that pool of clear, fresh water. Oh, and you are not a jerk. If anything, I've earned that award fair and square."

"You aren't making any sense. Other than Carolyn and Maribel wanting to continue to explore uh, I don't know quite how to put it."

"Carolyn believes the whole sock on the door thing is stupid and on that we happen to agree. She wants to spend the night with Maribel. Apparently, she really likes her. Sure, I think the primary focus will be hot sex because she also made it clear they aren't heading down the aisle anytime soon. But I get the sense they'd make a good pair. Carolyn isn't ruling that out in the future."

Joey kept blinking her eyes and probably looked shell-shocked to Sabrina. She was amazed that Sabrina hadn't asked the important question of why they didn't take their party to Maribel's. She opened her mouth to speak and then decided to twirl her hand in the air, gesturing for Sabrina to continue.

Sabrina leaned toward Joey and brought her hands around Joey's back pulling the two of them together as she licked her lips and then pressed them against Joey's. Joey's automatic response was to surrender to the gentle probing, causing the kiss to gather intensity. Before Joey knew it, her hips were rocking against Sabrina's and she wanted nothing more than to remove her clothes and move against Sabrina. Her heart raced and Joey was unsure of how to proceed. She didn't want to make a terrible misstep again. Sabrina broke the kiss and her hands moved to Joey's shirt as she slowly undid each button.

"Actions speak louder than words. Not that this isn't incredibly hot, you know, undressing you and making love against a wall...but I think it looks a lot more fun in the movies. Can we take our party to the bed, please?"

Stunned, Joey nodded. She was afraid to break the spell or ask for an explanation. Her shirt hung open revealing a simple, white, sports bra. Joey allowed Sabrina to seductively run her hand down her arm and pull her toward the bed.

"Are you sure?" Joey asked.

"I am. I'm so sorry about before. Right now, this is about us and nothing else. I want to make love with you not because I'm hurt, angry, or confused about Carolyn. It's like the Seattle fog has cleared and I can see for miles on top of a really high mountain. The view is breathtaking. You are breathtaking. You're everything I could ever hope for. You're kind, intelligent, funny, thoughtful, and incredibly sexy. I think I started falling for you that first time you smirked at me. Who knew there was such depth behind that cocky little grin of yours?" Sabrina sat on the edge of the bed.

Joey removed Sabrina's rain jacket, slipped it from her shoulders, and tossed the damp garment to the side of the bed. Sabrina's sweet scent soon replaced the slightly musky smell. "I admit your fine ass was something of a marvel, but I fell the minute I caught you scrutinizing my undies. I thought for sure you were about to sniff them. Then I got this crazy notion you harbored a secret desire to nick a pair."

Sabrina laughed as she brushed her fingers along Joey's jawline and kissed her neck. "Busted. I wanted to take a pair.

I thought you'd never miss one after I counted twenty-six pairs." Sabrina removed Joey's shirt as she continued her assault on Joey's neck.

"I knew right then and there we were kindred spirits and if we both ended up in jail for stealing panties, I'd die a happy woman as long as we went to the same penitentiary. We could be like the new Piper and Alex. I can't believe how addictive that love story is, in *Orange is the New Black*." Joey lifted Sabrina's shirt as Sabrina continued her assault on her neck. The rain of kisses left a sublime tingling all over her body. The feel of Sabrina's lips on her neck distracted her so much as they traveled down to the edge of her bra that she almost lost concentration, but she still unclasped Sabrina's bra. Muscle memory was all she had. She'd done this so many times before it was almost second nature to remove a woman's bra. Sabrina wasn't any woman. She was her future, and she wanted to make this last. She wanted this moment—her first time with Sabrina—to etch itself into her memory.

"Please tell me what you want. I don't want to leave anything to chance. Nothing short of perfection will do."

"Anything and everything feels nice right about now. It's been so long and I'm wound so tight, it won't take much for me to spin out of control."

"Good, because control is overrated. It's been a long time for me as well."

"Yeah, Carolyn shared that little secret with me. Seriously, Joey? No hook-ups since we met?" Sabrina stopped her kisses and leaned back capturing Joey's gaze.

Joey completely removed Sabrina's bra and reverently caressed her shoulders, neck, and breasts. "I told you that. I can't believe you thought I was lying. I was too busy trying to woo you although I didn't have the foggiest idea that was what I was doing until a few weeks ago."

"Ha, try not realizing things until a few days ago? Hey, are we going to talk or make love?" Sabrina joked.

"I am especially good at multi-tasking. Nothing turns me on more than doing both. Vocal lovers are a real plus."

Sabrina chuckled. "Even lovemaking is an intellectual experience to you."

"Not always, but with you that is a definite yes." Joey reached for the top button on Sabrina's jeans and popped it open with ease. She pulled down the zipper and grazed the soft cotton panties inside. Her touch caused Sabrina to gasp and Joey felt the slight dampness as she spread the clothing aside and tried to push her jeans down to remove them. "A little help, please?"

Sabrina lifted her rear, and that made it easy for Joey to liberate her jeans from her body.

"I won't even try to remove your bra. Those things make it impossible to be suave about undressing a person," Sabrina said.

Joey's hands had traveled down Sabrina's legs, but she quickly tugged on her sports bra, deftly removing it for Sabrina. She stood and removed her jeans so that all that remained as any kind of barrier was her own boi shorts and Sabrina's very sexy bikini briefs. Joey was bursting with excitement.

"If I remove these panties, you aren't going to slither out from under me in the middle of the night and try to stuff them in your jeans pocket, are you?" Joey grinned.

"Now where's the fun in making that promise. I won't ask you to agree to that if you don't expect me to either." Sabrina slowly removed her own underwear and Joey could see her rapt attention to where Joey was tossing her own boi shorts. Sabrina twirled her bikini in her finger and then laughed and sent it flying. After scooting up on the bed she motioned for Joey to join her. Joey imagined she might look like one of those caricatures panting after the hot woman. She crawled her way on top of Sabrina and their naked bodies came together and she could feel Sabrina's soft skin underneath her. The tickle of her small triangle of hair so close to her own sent Joey's arousal into space. She felt like she was flying through the air. Exhilarated and tense, they beautifully melded together and she moved on top of Sabrina. She shifted enough to delve her fingers into Sabrina's silky wet folds. With the barest touch she teased Sabrina who was squirming underneath her.

"You are driving me crazy," Sabrina whispered.

"Keep talking, tell me what you want."

"Can you go inside, but go slow."

Joey peppered Sabrina's shoulder with kisses as she pushed one finger inside while brushing her thumb against Sabrina's clit. Sabrina's hips rose to meet Joey and Joey expertly slid her finger in and out. The rhythm took on a frantic pace as Sabrina bucked beneath her and Joey could feel how close to the edge Sabrina was getting.

"Oh, oh, I'm so close, please don't stop."

"I know, sweetheart, I know. Let go. Let me feel you." One last slow thrust and Joey heard Sabrina cry out at the same time she felt Sabrina's vagina close all around her finger. Carefully she pulled out and moved down Sabrina's body so she could have her first taste.

"Are you trying to turn me into a bowl of Jell-O?" Sabrina stopped talking when Joey started to suck her clit. She moaned in what Joey hoped was delight.

Alternating between sucking and long strokes of her tongue all along Sabrina's folds, Joey brought Sabrina quickly to her second orgasm. Maintaining her connection to Sabrina, Joey slithered up to kiss Sabrina and flip her over so that Sabrina was lying on top of her. "Don't do anything yet. I want to feel your body on top of mine for a few minutes." She continued to stroke Sabrina's back as Sabrina lay on top of her with her head on Joey's shoulder. This kind of sensual closeness was the next best thing to the physical manifestation of love that Joey ever experienced. And it was in this moment she decided not to hold back.

"I love you, Sabrina."

Joey felt the moisture against her shoulder and wasn't sure what to think of the tears when she heard Sabrina's response, "I love you too."

It didn't matter they still had a lot to talk about, including Joey's eventual move to Forks and making it through the rest of medical school while maintaining a relationship. Right at this moment, everything was perfect. The rest was simply logistics.

CHAPTER EIGHTEEN

Being a light sleeper all her life, Sabrina carefully slipped out from under Joey's protective embrace. For most of the night Joey's long arm was draped over Sabrina's stomach. When she had moved it, Joey made small mewling sounds. Sabrina thought she might wake up, but she only shifted and turned over. Maybe she had only pretended to still be asleep, knowing what Sabrina was about to do. That wasn't out of the realm of possibility considering that's exactly what Joey had done less than an hour ago.

The room was still dark when Joey had made her move earlier in the night. Sabrina wondered if she possessed a smidgen of cat DNA to enable her to see in the pitch black. Like a heat-seeking missile, Joey had tiptoed to the area of her apartment where Sabrina had flung her panties several hours before they'd surrendered to exhaustion. After hours of making love, they had talked about everything, including when they might make another trip to Forks. Sabrina couldn't see Joey steal her panties, but she heard her feeling around on the floor and then making her way into the bathroom. She imagined that Joey would use the toilet as an excuse for why she'd left the warm bed in the middle of the night. The ruse wasn't going to fool either of them. And yet, that was the same falsity Sabrina decided she would mumble if Joey tried to tease her by calling her out on her crime.

This time taking a pair of panties wasn't as easy as stuffing them in her bra. She was crawling around the floor letting her senses take over. As she came across the various pieces of clothing, she tried to allow her hands to finger the garments and determine what they were. Finally, she came to a soft cotton cloth and explored the edges. She believed she had her prize. With the panties clutched in one hand, she quickly made her way to the bathroom and shut the door behind her so she could turn on the light. Her heart was pounding as she felt against the wall for the light switch. She held the boi shorts in front of her face for inspection and smiled as she saw the *Captivated* cover staring back at her. This was one of her favorite pairs. Now all she had to do was crawl around and find her rain jacket. She planned on stuffing the undies in the pocket and then making a quick getaway in the morning. She could use the excuse she needed to head back to her apartment to get ready for her early clinic day. She would offer to make dinner for Joey and they could talk more about their newly formed relationship and the agreed-upon rules.

The material on Sabrina's jacket was easy enough to distinguish from the other clothing. Within minutes of exiting the bathroom, Sabrina had successfully hidden the stolen panties in the zippered pocket. Lifting the covers, she slipped back into bed and spooned Joey who was now on her side turned in the opposite direction from before when Sabrina had been the small spoon.

"Everything okay?" Joey mumbled.

"Perfect." Sabrina made small circles on Joey's stomach. "Go back to sleep. I think we have a few more hours before I have to leave."

"You can take a shower here if you want," Joey groggily replied.

"Shh." Sabrina continued to caress Joey and felt her breathing return to the hypnotic pattern of someone who'd fallen back to sleep.

†

Joey opened her eyes and sighed in contentment as she felt Sabrina's body against her back. She remembered Sabrina making her move in the middle of the night and almost started laughing. She was sure neither one of them were under the illusion that the other didn't know exactly what they'd both done. Without either one of them saying a word, they'd clearly established the rules of the game. Joey would pretend she didn't know Sabrina had spent several minutes crawling along her apartment floor to find her discarded panties and Sabrina would offer her the same.

She had enough time before her alarm went off to fret over whether Sabrina would freak out or accept the redefinition of their relationship. She thought it was a fifty-fifty chance it could go either way. Joey wouldn't have too long to wait because she sensed that time was fast approaching. The cocoon of utter joy and peace was about to be disturbed.

The obnoxious blare of her smartphone alarm startled her. Sabrina groaned causing a tickle of air against Joey's neck. She turned to face Sabrina and such a swell of love overwhelmed her as she took in the slightly disheveled appearance. Parts of her hair were mashed up against her head and it was positively adorable to Joey.

"Morning. Did you sleep okay?"

Sabrina yawned and then stretched. "Wonderfully." Sabrina seemed to eye Joey carefully. "Joey, get that worried look off your face. I don't regret a single thing about last night. What I do regret is having to leave this comfortable bed, but I have to get ready for work. Although I'd like nothing better than to stay, take a leisurely shower, and dress for work in your apartment, all my clothes are at my place. I'll have to disturb the other lovebirds. Unfortunately, I don't have much time. Gotta scoot. But I'll make dinner for us tonight. Okay?"

Sabrina tossed off the covers and grabbed her jeans and shirt throwing them over her body. She made a showing of looking for her underwear and then grabbed her bra and stuffed it into her jacket.

"I understand. I'll bring the wine. What time should I come by?" Joey pulled herself up and leaned against the headboard.

"How 'bout fiveish? Will you be back from the ED by then?"

"Uh huh." Joey rubbed her eyes and yawned.

Sabrina walked to the bed with her jacket slung over her arm and caressed Joey's cheek before leaning down and placing a gentle kiss on her lips. "I still love you this morning. That hasn't changed in the bright daylight."

A broad smile appeared on Joey's lips. "Thank God, because I'm still mad for you."

Although Sabrina rushed out of her apartment, Joey was delighted with the turn of events. She hurried to find Sabrina's bikini briefs that she had squirreled away. They would occupy a place of honor in her special underwear drawer. In fact, she considered tossing away all the others and only keeping Sabrina's. Perhaps that was a symbol of her new outlook on life and love. Maybe she would share that with Sabrina someday and they could have a good laugh about it. She'd need to do her own laundry to keep up the pretense they'd established of feigning ignorance to both of their petty crimes. Joey liked to think she had an influence on this playful side to Sabrina.

†

Sabrina was humming all the way to her apartment. After bursting through the door she called out, "Carolyn and Maribel, you better cover your naked butts because I'm coming in. Sorry to interrupt, but I have to gather my work clothes and then you can return to whatever you were doing." Sabrina snickered. "Even if that was sleeping," she added. There was a small evil part of her that enjoyed waking them up. Especially since they'd made her bed the center of their little love affair.

When she didn't hear a response, she was curious. "Carolyn," she yelled louder. Crickets. "Hmm that's odd."

Not caring if they were still in bed, Sabrina barged into the bedroom, her bedroom, and found a neatly made bed. Not

213

a thing was out of place. The panic rose before she remembered that Carolyn often took the early shift at the coffeehouse and that was probably where she'd gone to. Although, she wasn't expecting Maribel up this early. Maribel was far from an early riser.

Finally, Sabrina's brain began to fire on all cylinders and the question she should have asked last night surfaced. Why in the world would Carolyn and Maribel need to remain in her apartment, in her bed? *What the hell?* Maribel had a perfectly good bed in her apartment and it was just down the hall. Sabrina had been so emotional and singularly driven when she finally recognized how much she would sacrifice if she didn't go for it with Joey. Needing that tiny extra push from Carolyn must have been the key.

Her joyous mood turned contemplative. What if they were all in it from the start? Creating this elaborate scenario to engineer everything that happened last night. God, maybe she had made a complete fool of herself. Did Joey really love her? Did she put Maribel and Carolyn up to this? Sabrina shook her head.

"No, Joey wouldn't do that. She's not like that."

Sabrina paced the room. She didn't have time for any of this. She'd talk with all of them tonight. And yet, sending a short text to Joey seemed like a good idea as she stripped and jumped into the shower.

Rushing around her apartment and quickly putting on her make-up, she left herself several extra minutes before she had to leave to catch the bus. Her phone was in her jacket pocket where she left it last night amongst the drama. She groaned, wondering if it still had a charge. Unzipping the pocket, she retrieved her phone and fired off a quick text to Joey.

214

Why did they ask me to stay at your place? What's wrong with Maribel's apartment?

Sabrina thought those were innocent enough questions. Not accusatory. Although interpreting text messages was dicey sometimes. She wondered if she should have called. In her line of work, jumping to conclusions was always a dangerous thing. For all she knew, Maribel's apartment might be in the middle of fumigation for some unwanted pest. She shuddered at that thought.

The contemplative smiley appeared on her phone followed by a Don't know. I was not going to interrupt anything last night with an unimportant question. A smiley with a wide grin punctuated the end of her reply. Does it really matter? Do you need me to walk you to the bus before I head to the hospital?

The smileys were something new. Sabrina wondered if Joey was trying extra hard to do something she thought Sabrina might appreciate. She wasn't impressed. Smiley faces were not her thing. She'd tell Joey that when they talked later.

No, I'll talk to you tonight. I was just wondering. You didn't have anything to do with this, did you?

Joey's response was instantaneous. *No*

She followed quickly with, Subversive tactics are not my style, except when it comes to stealing underwear. Another emoji ended the text.

Okay this last smiley helped emphasize that she was teasing. Despite thinking this was all a big conspiracy manufactured for her own good, Sabrina had to smile at Joey's last response. She wondered why she was making such a big deal of it, anyway. Exiting her apartment, she came face to face with Joey leaning on the wall outside her door.

"Hey, I thought I would wait for you. It was hard to determine your mood from the text. Worse form of communication, ever. I wanted to make sure you weren't upset."

"I'm not. Well, maybe a little. I'd hate to think our relationship started with a falsehood. By the way, smiley faces? Really?"

Joey looked sheepish. "They seemed like a good idea at the time. No emojis in the future. Got it."

"I like that there is still so much more to learn about one another."

"Definitely." Joey stroked Sabrina's face before kissing her. An almost chaste kiss that felt like a love punch.

Sabrina knew deep down the feelings behind that sweet gesture were anything but false and it settled her enough to let her insecurities go for now. "That was nice."

"Sabrina, I think you know there is nothing false about my feelings for you and I hope the same is true for you." A sad smile formed on Joey's face.

Sabrina looped her arm into Joey's and pulled her along the hallway needing to feel the fresh air rather than the claustrophobia of the dingy white walls in the stale enclosure. She hadn't paid much attention before to the hallways. They were merely an avenue to go from place A to place B. The industrial beige carpet was threadbare in numerous spots and she noticed a few large stains, probably coffee, but it was possible the stains were something far more disgusting like vomit. She hurried her steps.

"You know what I'm looking forward to?"

Joey tilted her head and made a face before chuckling. "I cannot keep up with your train of thought. What, please tell me, because now I am dying to know?"

"Moving out of this run-down apartment building. That hallway is the most depressing thing."

"Okay. A house with lots of light and bright cheery fixtures it is. As long as you are there with me, where we live doesn't matter. You know, when I make the big bucks, we'll have our pick of houses."

"Slow down. Who says I'm going to come live with you in vampireland? Besides, I'll probably have to continue to live in a dreary place while I pay off my massive school loans. Not everyone can get a hospital to offer a debt-free life after medical school."

"Ah, but that is where you are wrong. The behavioral health clinic attached to the hospital could set you up. Remember, Forks is one of those underserved populations. The hospital *and* clinics are eligible for state and federal loan repayment programs. One is seventy thousand, and the other is seventy-five thousand. You would qualify and I know they are interested in you."

"You have this all worked out, don't you?" Sabrina asked.

"The bigger question is why don't you? You're the definition of methodical." Joey grinned.

The two women reached the bus stop and Sabrina kissed Joey then pushed her. "Go, you don't want to be late for your clerkship."

"Still love you," Joey called over her shoulder as she walked away.

"Yeah, yeah, me too." Sabrina waved her hand in the air and smiled.

CHAPTER NINETEEN

Two plastic bags weighed Sabrina down as she juggled them while opening her apartment. She was running late and wanted to start dinner before Joey arrived. Garlic and other delectable herbs assaulted her senses the minute she opened the door. Carolyn was in the kitchen chopping something that Sabrina couldn't quite make out.

"Oh, um, I was going to make dinner for Joey." She walked into the kitchen and looked at the sizzling garlic in the pan. Tiny pieces of diced tomato sat on the cutting board. Sabrina set her bags on the counter.

Carolyn stopped her chopping, began unloading the groceries and putting them away. "Sit and relax. I'm making a special meal for the two of you. It's kind of a belated thank you. I bought wine and I promise I haven't partaken in any,

218

only needed a tiny bit for the meal. I'll pour you a glass and there should be plenty enough left for the two of you. I'm heading to Maribel's tonight after I prepare the meal. I'm going to steal two plates for us, but I'm making enough for an army."

"Okay. Speaking of heading to Maribel's, why did you need to stay here last night instead of going to her place?" Sabrina sat on the stool in front of the kitchen counter.

Carolyn winced and then turned to retrieve a wineglass from the cupboard. "Oh, uh, I guess it finally dawned on you that nothing about that request for you to stay at Joey's made sense. I know, I took advantage of your rapidly shifting emotions. You never were very logical or clear thinking whenever you were hurt, frustrated, angry, or confused. Took you long enough to figure it out."

"That's just it. I haven't quite figured it out."

"Honestly, I had my doubts it would work, but I suppose subliminal desire is powerful. You needed a little push. Maribel and I gave it to you." Carolyn filled the wineglass she set in front of Sabrina. Wiping her hands on the dishtowel, she placed one on top of Sabrina's as they rested on the counter. "I want you to be happy. You are with Joey. I saw it, Maribel saw it. We kind of cooked up a plan. So sue me, sometimes I'm devious. In this case, it was for your own good."

"Was the whole desperate phone call also part of your brilliant plan?"

Carolyn held up her hands in supplication. "That was definitely more Maribel's idea than mine. She figured if you didn't rush right back to be by my side, then you and Joey were meant to be. A kind of forced choice. I didn't like it at first, but I kinda had to know, too. I don't blame you for not

219

coming back to rescue me, on the contrary, that told me you were ready to move on. But I know you, and you still needed a tiny little push in the right direction. Don't be mad."

"I'm not mad, but please don't do that again."

"Just for a clarification, I did smoke a little weed, but I didn't have the kind of reaction Maribel described. She's quite the little actress, huh?"

"Did you two plan on having me catch you in bed?"

Carolyn blushed. "Um, no, that part was unexpected. Neither one of us wanted to hurt you. Things sort of evolved between the two of us. Before we knew it, we were hot and heavy with one another. She stayed with me until I came down from a stupendous high. I'm still trying to explore the consequences of that walk on the wild side with my therapist. There might be a difference of opinion on the matter."

"Well, I'll let you figure that out with the professionals in that area of expertise. I'm not a drug counselor so I plan to stay out of that part of your life. I've turned over a new leaf. Maybe that will start a trend and it'll rub off on Maribel."

"I suppose what we cooked up wasn't the smartest plan, but it worked. Maribel's ways are sometimes more effective than brutal honesty. She's not as bad as you think."

"I never said she was, but it figures. She's all about the games, all about the games, all about the games..." Sabrina sang to the melody of the song, *All About the Bass*.

"I am so impressed with this whimsical side of you. Sing it, sister." Carolyn laughed. "Maybe I like a little game-playing here and there. It worked, didn't it? Please tell me the two of you fucked like little bunnies last night."

"So crude. I am not going to kiss and tell. Let's just say we came to a mutual agreement."

"Oh, for fuck's sake, you sound like you entered into some boring ass contract."

"Ugh, God I do, don't I? Why in the world would someone like Joey fall in love with me?"

"Because, underneath all that rubble is a kind, caring, intelligent, funny, and dare I say cheeky, human being. Sabrina, you are easy to fall in love with and not so easy to fall out of love with. I should know. Been there, done that."

"I never meant to hurt you."

"You're apologizing to me? Oh, brother. That is truly the cherry on top. After all the shit I've put you through. Look, I'm not gonna lie, until I saw how happy you were when you were getting ready to go on that adventure with Joey to Forks, I harbored a small hope we might get back together. But I want you to really listen to what I have to say right now. Your happiness is far more important than some stupid illusion we might make it work. Besides, after yesterday, I kinda realized someone else might rock my world." Carolyn looked up when the knock on the door interrupted their discussion. "There's your princess charming."

Before answering the door, Sabrina walked around the island and kissed Carolyn on the cheek. "I don't regret what we had or my time with you. It wasn't always filled with heartache for either of us. We had some good times, didn't we?"

"We did." Carolyn pushed Sabrina towards the door. "Go, live, be happy. Move forward, never backward."

CHAPTER TWENTY

Joey smiled as she remembered the evening when those final barriers crumbled away and the possibility of developing a real relationship with Sabrina emerged from the rubble. She was eagerly waiting for her to arrive for their date. It was their one-year anniversary, and they had a lot to celebrate.

When the knock came on the door her smile widened. She was nervous and didn't want to push Sabrina, but they needed to figure things out. She was moving to Forks in less than a month and Sabrina hadn't, to Joey's knowledge, made a final decision on the offer the clinic had made to her. She seemed excited by the job offer, but there were still times Sabrina held her cards close to her chest. She'd also received a generous offer in Port Angeles which was only an hour away. At least she had narrowed her job search to locations that were a reasonable driving distance from Forks.

Joey hadn't graduated at the top of her class, which was her original plan, but she had passed her exams with flying colors. That was all that mattered. Not being number one was a sacrifice she'd gladly made and would do it again in a heartbeat. She also hadn't accepted any other residency that put her further away from Sabrina. The hospital had wanted her so badly, they'd created a residency program for her to complete her final two years in Forks.

Sabrina had finally decided to toss out the dissertation she'd started and replace it with her passion for exploring what she referred to as the fifth pane. Her professors weren't jumping for joy, but she'd convinced them she would never have the motivation to finish if she had to stick to her old topic. Everything was falling into place. Sabrina had completed her PhD program and Joey was heading to Forks where she hoped Sabrina would join her. Maribel and Carolyn were ready to take the plunge and move in together. Sabrina and Joey were both hopeful it would work for them, but if it didn't, it was neither one of their businesses to intercede.

Joey knew without a single doubt she wanted to marry Sabrina. Have a family with her. She wanted to raise her kids in a small town, not a big city. She wasn't sure if Sabrina shared that dream. Sometimes she talked like she did and then other times she was wistful about giving up the benefits of living in a city like Seattle.

Sabrina had that sexy grin on her face as she twirled a pair of panties in her fingers. "I've got the price of admittance right here. No more life of crime for you. See, I told you that once you entered into a serious, committed relationship your life of crime would stop."

Joey raised her eyebrow. "Funny. I continue to bare my soul to you, and this is the thanks I get. Mocking my former affliction."

"An affliction you passed along to me."

Joey grinned. "True dat. Come in, come in. I hope takeout is okay. Now that you have a chef in the making for your roommate, it's hard to compete." Joey pouted. "I know that's why you wouldn't move in with me. She's a better cook."

"You would have to actually cook for me for that to be true. And you know perfectly well why I made that decision. Please don't tell her this, but not every single one of her creations is a hit. It would crush her to hear that."

Joey shook her head. "You aren't doing any favors by not letting her know what works and what doesn't."

"I know, I know. I figure she gets that at school, I don't have to be the one to offer brutal honesty. Besides, she knows. Apparently, I have the kind of face that is totally transparent. I'll never win at poker."

Joey laughed. "No, you won't. I knew what was in your head when you were holding up my undies that first day." She waggled her eyebrows. "What I had no idea about was how inventive you are. Now that totally blew me away. It's always the quiet, deliberate, and careful ones who are the wildest in bed."

Sabrina smacked Joey lightly on the chest and made a beeline to the bag sitting on the coffee table. She eagerly opened the bag and peered inside. "What did you bring me?"

"Thai. Extra bland. Just for you. I never could understand how you can love Thai food, yet hate anything with the slightest punch to it. Thai is synonymous with spicy."

"No, it isn't. And our favorite place knows how I like it."

"Well, of course they do. You've only given them detailed instructions like twenty times on your aversion to anything too spicy. I think they got it after the first three times we went there."

"Why are you being purposely mean to me? Is this about the fact I haven't told you which job I took?" Sabrina walked into the kitchen to retrieve the chopsticks, placing them on the coffee table next to the takeout containers.

And there it was. Out in the open, her biggest fear that Sabrina might not want to live with her, much less marry. Joey had convinced herself that if Sabrina took the job in Port Angeles, which was a message she did not want to listen to, it would mean she wasn't all that serious about Joey. At least not in the same way that Joey was planning their future in her head.

"Oh, God. I am such an asshole." Joey walked over and grabbed Sabrina's hand.

"No, you're not. I know how much this decision affects you...us," she amended.

"I can't help having this whole vision of what our future would be like. Together. And that doesn't include living in separate towns."

"It doesn't?" Sabrina teased.

Joey's heart pounded. She wasn't sure she would like what Sabrina had to say. She was teasing her. Maybe that was her way of lightening the mood before the hammer came down. "Are you going to tell me what you decided or not? Put me out of my misery, please," Joey begged.

Sabrina pulled Joey into a tight hug. "Oh hon, don't you know I only applied for that job in Port Angeles because I didn't want to put all my eggs in one basket. Just because you were convinced I had the Forks job in the bag, didn't necessarily make it so."

"For someone so smart, how could you not see they were positively salivating over the possibility of a twofer."

"A twofer?" Sabrina asked.

"Yeah recruiting two highly trained professionals instead of one."

"And you believe it makes no difference we're a couple?"

"None at all. You do know the HR Director is a lesbian?" Joey placed a quick kiss on her lips.

"Get out. Really? She doesn't look like a lesbian." Sabrina broke from Joey's embrace and stared at her.

"Seriously. You did not actually utter those words, did you? What does a lesbian look like?"

"You know, I get a vibe. Admit it, don't you have that gaydar thing? The intense eye contact. A subtle kind of checking another woman out," Sabrina explained.

"She's old enough to be our mother and happily married. I don't think those two clues apply in that situation," Joey responded.

"They don't?"

"No, and I don't check out every new woman who maintains eye contact with me a second or two longer than necessary." Joey put her hands on her hips and gave Sabrina the stink eye.

"You do too. You did it with me."

"Well yeah, that was before we fell madly in love with each other. Now I only have eyes for you." Joey puckered her lips and made kissing sounds.

"Sweet talker."

"You haven't told me your decision yet."

"Of course I took the Forks job. Let's go house hunting this weekend!"

Joey picked Sabrina up and spun her around. "Really? Are you sure? Are we buying or renting?"

Sabrina smiled. "Not sure yet, you know I'll need to process this more. We should tell the real-estate agent to show us all the options."

"Hey, by the way, I talked to Annabelle the other evening. She has some new panties she made." Joey wiggled her eyebrows. "She wants to have us over for dinner some weekend when her wife is visiting."

"Joey Hartford, we are not going to steal another pair of panties from that sweet woman."

"Why not?"

"Because we are entering a phase in adulthood where stealing has no place. Setting a good example for our children is going to be important."

"Our children?" Joey's grin widened. "You've thought about having children with me?"

"Of course I have. Haven't you?"

"Every single day since the first time we made love. How many?" Joey grabbed Sabrina's hand again and led her to the couch. Casual dining was the way they'd always done things, and it worked for them. She wasn't about to change it up now and try to create an atmosphere of romance that didn't fit the two of them.

"How many what?" Sabrina poured from the open bottle of wine sitting on the coffee table and filled both glasses.

"How many children were you thinking we should have?"

"No more than two. I heard they were a lot of work," Sabrina joked.

"Two it is. Maybe we should get married first. I wouldn't want to raise a couple of bastards. Forks may be liberal enough to accept a lesbian couple, but I think they might want us to be married before children come along."

"Bull crap and you know it. Is this your lame attempt at a proposal?" Sabrina lifted her glass of wine and motioned for Joey to do the same.

"Okay, no. So...if this was a proposal, not that I'm saying it is or anything...but what would be your answer?"

"God, you can be so dense sometimes. Yes, of course. I want something special for a proposal though. You need to put that thinking cap on. I better feel like I am the center of your universe after you propose."

"Trust me, you are." Joey lifted her glass in the air.

"And for further clarification, that doesn't mean some engineered romantic evening with candles and roses. We don't do that. I want ingenuity. I love you, Joey Hartford, famed panty thief." She touched her glass to Joey's.

"I love you more, Sabrina Maxwell. And if ingenuity is what you want, that's what you'll get, even if I have to steal it from someone."

"I guess being a panty thief and a thief of hearts isn't enough for you. You have to always be number one, don't you?"

Joey laughed and sipped her wine.

ABOUT THE AUTHOR

ANNETTE MORI

Annette is an award-winning author, published by Affinity Rainbow Publications, who lives in the beautiful Pacific Northwest with her wife and their five furry kids. With nineteen published novels and the Goldie Award for her fourth novel, *Locked Inside,* she finally feels like a real author. Annette is as much a reader as a writer and is always looking for the next lesfic novel to queue up. She came up with the One Fan at a Time tagline, because it rolled off the tongue much better than One Reader at a Time. After pondering who she was at her core, it was all about connecting to each reader on a personal level. Annette would be the first to admit she doesn't do well with the masses. If someone picks up her book and it touches them, she believes she has achieved what she wants with her writing by reaching each reader. It is who she is at her core. Drop her a line, she loves to hear from readers: annettemori0859@gmail.com.

Sign up for her mailing list: http://eepurl.com/cS7nr9
Check out her blog: Everyday Occurrences:
https://annettemori0859.wordpress.com/
Visit the Affinity Rainbow Publications website for her books and those of many other outstanding authors:
https://www.affinityebooks.com

OTHER AFFINITY BOOKS

<u>Before the Light</u> by Samantha Hicks
One year after, her long-time partner Meredith's abduction, and their subsequent break-up, Kathleen Bowden-Scott's life is spiralling out of control. She meets Bethany Jones and despite an instant attraction Kathleen shies away. In this fast-paced, romantic suspense, lies are exposed and hearts unite as Kathleen and Beth fight for their future.

<u>Wanted for Christmas</u> by JM Dragon
Belle Farrow knew what she wanted for Christmas–work. She had little to offer but a minor degree in cookery and household management. certainly not enough for a decent chef or housekeeper position. Then she saw an advert in the local newspaper. Wanted: Housekeeper/cook/nanny for the period of Christmas until the New Year. This is Christmas. Perhaps Santa reads the ad column too and pushes a little spirit of the season to that request.

<u>Dreams in a Jar</u> by JM Dragon
When you believe your life is a never-ending spiral of despair and the only personal joy you have is inside of a novel, would you grab a chance to hide away in the local bookstore and dream of adventures? Thea's life is about to embark on a journey she never envisioned when local bookstore owner, Marion, is taken ill. Her niece, Sheryl Appleby, takes over the reins and her presence provides Thea the courage to take a leap of faith. Can she embrace the butterfly effect, or are Thea's dreams bottled in a jar forever?

<u>Pleasure Workers</u> by Annette Mori
Alex Cortez is accomplished at two things, fixing broken equipment and pleasuring women. She is happily doing both at the Ranch in Nevada. Danna Nichols, newly widowed, feels lost and alone. When her good friend Lindy invites her to check out the newly established Trophy Wives Club, it awakens dormant feelings and desires. An instant attraction happens and the two form a bond under unlikely circumstances. Will the challenges of their social status tear them apart before they can enjoy the pleasures of their new love?

<u>The Trophy Wives Club</u> by Ali Spooner
What happens when under-appreciated professional women are offered their dream jobs? When one of Atlanta's elite businesswomen and wife of a prominent judge sets her sights on a goal, life begins to change for these women. Friendships and romance bloom in a unique fitness club on the outskirts of Atlanta, where more than a workout is offered.

Unknown Forces by Samantha Hicks
Jennifer Wilson spent the last seventeen years raising her younger sister Kelsey after a boating accident killed their parents. Riley hasn't had an easy life either and her friendship with Kelsey is the only thing steadfast in her life. When tragedy and secrets emerge, Jennifer and Riley must learn to lean on each other. The growing attraction between them only complicates matters. When events conspire to keep them apart, will they trust the unknown forces that keep pushing them together, or hide from their feelings forever?

A Window to Love by Annette Mori
Two life events, two paths colliding, two souls destined to meet. Mandie Carter lives an uninspired life. No passion, no romance, and just when she thought things couldn't get worse, life throws her a curve. Gail Forrester is barely hanging on. Buried under mountains of debt, only her much in demand architectural designs keep her afloat. Now, they must find a way forward together through what life and destiny has in store for them. Only then can they hope to step into that window to love.

Free Spirit by Erica Lawson
Priory McAllister has fought off boardroom sharks, handled high-pressure jobs, and thought she'd seen it all. She found her dream home and couldn't wait to move in. Unknown to Priory, two ghosts...Rhee and a mischievous Dylan...have inhabited the house since 1935. They have no intention of leaving. Jacey Ryder, Priory's long-suffering secretary, gets to play referee between her boss and a bossy ghost, as each side try to lay claim to the house. What can she do when an unstoppable force, (her boss) meets an immovable object,

(the ghost) besides hope for a peaceful solution? They are like two peas in a pod—two angry, stubborn peas in a pod.

Addicted to You by Erin O'Reilly
Elin Prescot's dream to be a top fashion designer is finally within her reach—then Marissa Banks enters her life. Snared by her first taste of passion, Elin is consumed by desire for more. Her life spirals out of control until she meets Doctor Aimee Sullivan, who understands all too well what Elin is going through. Can Elin let Aimee into her heart? Or will her addiction keep her enthralled with Marissa? This story explores first love, intense passion, manipulation of emotions, and the gentleness of real love and true romance.

At Last by JM Dragon
A perfume company in trouble, leading to a town in peril. Old Loves. Unrequited Loves. New passions. Can the reclusive Gene Desrosiers save her family company and the people she cares for, even though some are not aware of it yet? Will an ultimate sacrifice win the day, or will Grady end up a ghost town of unfulfilled lives? This love story will warm your heart.

Deuce by Jen Silver
When Jay Reid was in her twenties, she had it all. A professional tennis career, Charlotte, the love of her life and a new baby. Charlotte's research vessel, RV Caspian, was lost at sea, leaving Jay to raise their child alone. Rescued by a local fisherman, with no memory of her life before, she lives on the Faroe Islands as Katrin Nielsen. Seeing a beached seal one day triggers her memory. Twenty-three years is a long time. Is the love they once shared strong

enough to be rekindled or have too many years passed eroding all hope of a happy ever after?

After Dark by Samantha Hicks

Can a love that starts out in terror be real or last? Meredith Ashcroft disappears on her way to a client meeting. Five months later, art gallery manager Stephanie Edwards is also held and tortured by the same sadistic man. Thrown together trying to overcome their shared ordeal, they find themselves falling in love. Is it true love or just an attachment to each other born out of fear for their lives?

Affinity
Rainbow Publications

eBooks, Print, Free eBooks

Visit our website for more publications available online.

www.affinityrainbowpublications.com

Published by Affinity Rainbow Publications
A Division of Affinity eBook Press NZ LTD
Canterbury, New Zealand

Registered Company 2517228

www.ingramcontent.com/pod-product-compliance
Lightning Source LLC
Chambersburg PA
CBHW071145260626
47162CB00003B/924